THE GUGGENHEIM MYSTERY

THE GUGGENHEIM MYSTERY

ROBIN STEVENS

BASED ON AN IDEA AND CHARACTERS BY SIOBHAN DOWD

ALFRED A. KNOPF 🐕 NEW YORK

Visit us on the Web! rhcbooks.com

Educators and librarians, for a variety of teaching tools, visit us at RHTeachersLibrarians.com

Library of Congress Cataloging-in-Publication Data
Name: Stevens, Robin, author.
Title: The Guggenheim mystery / Robin Stevens ; based on an idea and characters by Siobhan Dowd.
Description: First American edition. | New York : Alfred A. Knopf, 2018. | Originally published: London : Penguin Random House UK, 2017. | Sequel to: The London Eye mystery. | Summary: While visiting their cousin Salim in New York City, Ted and Kat investigate the theft of a famous painting from the Guggenheim Museum for which Salim's mother is the prime suspect.
Identifiers: LCCN 2018006128 (print) | LCCN 2018014293 (ebook) | ISBN 978-0-525-58235-9 (trade) | ISBN 978-0-525-58236-6 (lib. bdg.) | ISBN 978-0-525-58237-3 (ebook)
Subjects: | CYAC: Asperger's syndrome—Fiction. | Stealing—Fiction. | Brothers and sisters—Fiction. | Cousins—Fiction. | Solomon R. Guggenheim Museum—Fiction. | New York (N.Y.)—Fiction. | Mystery and detective stories. | BISAC: JUVENILE FICTION / Mysteries & Detective Stories. | JUVENILE FICTION / Family / Siblings. | JUVENILE FICTION / People & Places / United States / General.
Classification: LCC PZ7.S84555 (ebook) | LCC PZ7.S84555 Gug 2018 (print) | DDC [Fic]—dc23

Printed in the United States of America
October 2018
10 9 8 7 6 5 4 3 2 1

First American Edition

TO SIOBHAN, FOR THIS MYSTERY.

AND TO DAVID, FOR NEW YORK.

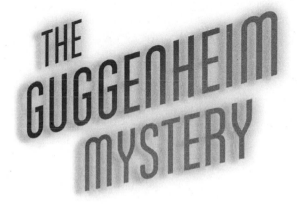

1

PATTERNS

Here are some facts about me.

My name is Ted Spark.

I am twelve years and 281 days old.

I have seven friends.

There are nine lies in the silver folder labeled MY LIES that I keep in my desk drawer.

I am going to be a meteorologist when I grow up, so I can help people when the weather goes wrong. This is something that will happen more and more in the future. The world is heating up because of increasing levels of greenhouse gases in the atmosphere. This is causing the seas to rise, and weather to become more extreme and unpredictable. This is very interesting and also very concerning. I don't know why the rest of my family—Mum and Dad and my sister, Kat—are not as worried about this as I am.

It might have something to do with my funny brain, which works on a different operating system than other people's. It makes patterns like the weather very important to me, and makes me notice things that no one else could. I see the way things connect, and I connect things that other people do not seem able to. I am learning that there are even patterns in stories and myths and poetry. There are patterns everywhere you look.

Three months ago I solved the mystery of how my cousin Salim disappeared from a pod on the London Eye Ferris wheel while Kat and I were watching him. A man came up to us while we were queuing and offered us a free ticket, which Salim took. Salim got into the pod that went up at 11:32 a.m. on Monday, May 24, but when it came down again at 12:02 p.m., we did not see him get out. Mum and Dad and Aunt Gloria, who is Mum's sister and Salim's mum, thought that his disappearance was impossible. Even the police thought it was impossible.

But I knew that even though some things seem impossible, they always make sense once you understand them. For example, in the year 1700 there was an earthquake in America that caused a tsunami in Japan, 4,721 miles away. A tsunami is a huge wave. At that time, the Japanese people who were hit by it probably didn't even know that America existed, but the tsunami flattened their houses anyway. This is absolutely true, and it proves that the whole of history is a pattern, and everything is caused by something else.

When Salim disappeared, Kat and I came up with nine possible theories, and one of them had to be true. That is what I knew, and that is what Kat and I proved. We worked out which theory was correct, and we got Salim back, and then he and Aunt Gloria went to New York together, to a new weather system and a new life, and a new job for Aunt Gloria as a curator at the Guggenheim Museum (my encyclopedia says that a curator is someone who looks after paintings and pieces of art, and organizes exhibitions in art galleries). But we were still part of that life, and when Kat and Mum and I went to visit them during our summer holiday this year, the mystery of the London Eye turned out not to be the only mystery in our universe.

Fifteen days ago, on the first proper day of our holiday, a painting was stolen from the Guggenheim Museum.

When the painting was stolen, everyone kept saying that it was priceless. That was not correct. They should have said that it was worth $20 million in New York, which is £16.02 million if you are in London, where Kat and Mum and Dad and I live. (This is because of something called the *exchange rate*, which decides the number of dollars you can buy for a pound, or the other way round. The exchange rate isn't always the same, which I find very interesting.)

It was very difficult for me to understand how a painting could be worth so much. Unlike photographs, paintings are not always accurate or realistic. I can see why a photograph would be valuable, because it shows you what the photographer saw at the very moment the picture was taken. My cousin Salim loves photography, and his photographs helped us solve the mystery of his disappearance. When I look at his pictures, I can tell exactly how the world looked when he took them. It's like time travel. But paintings are not like that, and so at first I wasn't very interested in the stolen painting.

But then Aunt Gloria was blamed. The police thought that she had stolen it, and they tried to put her in prison. That would be bad for her, and also bad for Salim. Salim is my cousin and one of my seven friends, and so I knew that I had to help him by getting the painting back again, and proving that Aunt Gloria had not been the one to take it.

This is how I, and Kat and Salim, did it.

2

FIGURES OF SPEECH

Dad calls Aunt Gloria *Hurricane Gloria*. This is a good name for her. She leaves *a trail of destruction in her wake* (Dad's words). In fact, Aunt Gloria does not physically destroy things. She is just quite noisy and chaotic. Dad's name for her is an example of a *figure of speech*.

Dad has been teaching me about figures of speech, which are words or phrases that sound like they mean one thing, but really mean another. One example is *It's raining cats and dogs*. This doesn't mean that kittens and puppies are actually falling from the sky. It means it's raining hard. I am making progress with figures of speech, but I still get confused very easily.

I knew we were going to see Aunt Gloria and Salim in New York before I was meant to. On July 26, when I should have been asleep, I eavesdropped (which doesn't mean I dropped anything, it means that I listened carefully outside the living-room door when I wasn't supposed to) on a conversation between Mum and Dad. Mum and Aunt Gloria had just had a phone call, and Mum was telling Dad about it. Mum said that Aunt Gloria wanted us all to come and visit her and Salim in New York.

"I think she's missing me," said Mum. "The new job's going well so far—but you know how hard it was for her to get there." I did know, because New York is roughly 3,459 miles and one seven-hour-and-fifty-minute flight from London. "And Salim seems to be fitting in—isn't that a marvel? But it'd be nice for him to see his cousins. What do you think, love?"

Dad said he thought that it sounded like a lot of money, and Mum might take me and Kat but she couldn't count on him coming too, because *someone* had to hold down a job and earn the money for the mortgage and school uniforms and Ted's appointments. I felt the air pressure drop, and a cold front sweep into the living room. (This is a metaphor, another thing I am learning about. The temperature on our home thermostat by the stairs was seventeen degrees Celsius and it did not change.)

"Don't be like that, love," said Mum after a pause. "Glo and Salim are family. We have to stick together, especially after what happened in the spring. Just think of it—the children will love it! It'll be a holiday for them! And . . . it might be good for Kat."

Dad sighed. "It might," he said. "And Ted as well. He needs to start learning how to cope with the rest of the world."

The air in the living room metaphorically warmed, but an icy pocket formed around me as I sat on the stairs. I did not like hearing Dad say that. I was happy in London. I knew its geography and its weather. I knew the tube. I was not sure I wanted to travel to another country.

Last term at school I had learned about some journeys that made traveling sound dangerous and bad. When Christopher Columbus discovered America in 1492, he did it by mistake while he was looking for India. That journey took him a whole eight weeks. This is actually not much time at all compared to how long it took Odysseus, the legendary Greek hero, to cross the Mediterranean in

The Odyssey (ten years). Both these journeys reminded me how big and confusing the world can be, and how it is possible to get lost in it.

What if I got lost in New York? What if I never came home again?

3

THE HOME FRONT

To calm myself down, I decided to look up the Guggenheim Museum, where Aunt Gloria worked, in my encyclopedia. What I discovered made me feel a bit happier. The Guggenheim is an important New York landmark, just like the Statue of Liberty. *Museum* is not an entirely accurate word to describe it. My favorite museum in London, the British Museum, is big and hundreds of years old, and full of statues and jewels and pots. I like to go there and think about the patterns in history. But the Guggenheim is not like that. It was opened in 1959, so it's much newer than the British Museum. It also doesn't have any jewels, or pots. It is a museum that mostly just holds paintings. It is a very unusual museum, just like I am a very unusual person.

It was designed by Frank Lloyd Wright, a famous American architect, and when it first opened, it made a lot of people very upset. This is because Frank Lloyd Wright didn't want to design an ordinary square building with ordinary walls and floors and ceilings. Instead, he wanted his museum to be an interesting shape. So instead of square, it's round, with a round spiraling ramp inside it.

I was interested when I read about that. I thought that I would like to see a place so full of patterns.

But then I thought about who I was going with, and I felt worried all over again. What Dad had meant about Kat, but not said properly, because grown-ups are bad at finishing sentences, was that this summer she was being Mad, Mean Kat approximately 97 percent of the time. She had failed her math and science exams at the end of the year, and almost failed history, which made Mum and Dad very unhappy. "But it doesn't matter. I don't want to do any of them for GCSE," Kat had said when she opened her envelope from school. "I want to do art and design. And media studies."

"Absolutely not!" said Mum. "You know you have to

do math, it's the law. And as for art—Kat, love, you have to be sensible! Your father and I want you to study practical subjects. There'll be time for art later."

"But Auntie Glo's not practical," said Kat, sticking out her chin and fiddling with her hair. "She studied art, didn't she? I want to be like her."

"Your aunt's doing all right now, but she's struggled, Kat," said Mum, folding her arms. "The worry I've had over her career—love, there were years when she couldn't pay her way, and we had to help. I won't have that for you."

"That's just not *fair!*" yelled Kat, and that was the beginning of the argument.

Sometimes I don't understand people's emotions. But this time it was very easy. Everyone was angry. Our house was full of shouting and tears, which I imagined in my head as cold fronts and showers, for weeks. Kat stayed out late in the park with her friends, or came home on time but refused to leave her room for dinner. She also let her hair grow, so that Dad said she looked like a shaggy sheepdog, and cut it herself into a strange new shape that made Mum shout and Dad say, "Kat, absolutely not."

"All right, then, I'll get my belly button pierced," she said. And the hair was allowed to stay.

Kat began to spend a lot of time on Dad's computer in the evenings, the green light on her face making the bones of her cheeks stand out. Apparently, Kat is beautiful, but I don't know how anyone knows that. To me she just looks like Kat. The second time I caught her at the computer, she looked up and said, "Buzz off, Ted. I'm emailing my friend from school." Actually, she didn't say *buzz*, she said a much more awful word that Mum would have whacked her for, but I am translating.

I *had a hunch* (a figure of speech that means a deductive suspicion, not being crouched over) that this behavior was suspicious. I knew that the person Kat was emailing wasn't a friend from school. I knew this because Kat does not email her friends, she texts them. Her phone is always going off at the dinner table and making Dad say, "Put it away, Kat." She would only email someone she couldn't text. And the one person she knew who it would be too expensive to text, because he lived in the USA, was Salim.

What could Kat and Salim be emailing each other about?

* * *

Then, on August 1, Mum and Dad told Kat and me properly about us going with her to New York. "REALLY?" squealed Kat, making my ears hurt. She went whirling up to Mum and Dad and hugged them both, and then she tried to hug me. This was an easy emotion to understand: Kat was happy about going to New York. Then she ran to Dad's computer again and tapped away at it. Kat *was* emailing Salim, I thought. My deductions had been confirmed.

And I was upset, because even though Salim had been my friend too when he was in London, he had not emailed me at all—not since I had helped to solve the mystery of his disappearance. Was this because he liked Kat better now? Were they becoming better friends through the words of their emails, and leaving no room for me?

4

THE ODYSSEY, PART ONE

I thought about this more and more, and on the morning of our journey, Wednesday, August 8, I tried to talk to Mum about it. But she was too busy zipping shampoo bottles into plastic bags and saying, "Make sure you pack underpants, Kat! We'll be there for eight days— Oh, where is my good blouse?"

"Mum," I said. "I think Kat's doing something."

"Of course she is, Ted," said Mum. "She's packing. Thank heavens, for once I know what she's doing. Have you got your things?"

"Hrumm," I said carefully.

I had put my encyclopedia, my new alarm clock, my

radio, my toothbrush and two pairs of underwear into the suitcase Mum had laid out on my bed. On top I put my library copy of *The Odyssey*, which is the book about Odysseus's adventures. Mr. Shepherd at school gave it to me to read, and it seemed very suitable now that I was going on a long journey too.

But Mum got very upset when she saw my suitcase. "Ted, what about the rest of your clothes?" she cried.

I had to explain that I was going to wear my school uniform every day, like I always do.

"It'll be sweltering, Ted! You'll boil! And that radio won't work in Gloria's place in New York. American plugs are different—it's the electricity— Oh, Ted, love, don't look like that."

My head had gone to the side. I was imagining New York air boiling me like water in a pan, New York electricity frying the twisting circuits of my radio. What if I did not work there any more than my radio did?

And what if I could not cope without Dad there to help explain things to me when I did not understand them? This would be my first time going anywhere away from home without Dad, only with Mum and Kat.

When we arrived at our gate at Heathrow Airport and I saw the airplane that was about to shoot us all the way across the ocean, I became even more worried. Odysseus's boats keep on sinking in his story—sea travel is extremely dangerous—but I thought that I would still prefer a boat to the plane we were going to travel in. It didn't look as though it should be able to even get off the ground. I stepped backward.

"Come *on,* Ted!" shouted Kat, dancing away from us down the ramp that led to the plane. She was very excited. She wanted to get to New York, and Salim.

When the plane took off, it shook and rattled and shot upward so fast that I felt as though my stomach had (literally, and not metaphorically) been left behind. I covered my ears with my hands. The plane was a rattling tube, and I was shaking inside it.

"Look at the clouds!" said Mum. "It's all right, Ted."

I opened my eyes and looked. The clouds were below me. They were cumulus congestus clouds, because it had been a warm sunny day in London with a chance of rain. In Greek myths, which *The Odyssey* is part of, a god called Helios travels across the sky in the chariot of the sun, and that was how I was traveling, as fast and high as a god. But I was not sure that I felt like a god. I was still not sure that I was glad about this journey.

The plane rocked, and I groaned, but next to me Kat bounced, just like the plane.

At last the airplane rattled us down through the clouds, and into New York. New York's airport is called John F. Kennedy, after the president who was shot, and thinking that thought made me uncomfortable. When we came to the arrivals hall, everything in it smelled like metal, and I didn't know where to look. Even though we were back on the ground, there was a bad feeling still lodged in my esophagus.

Then Mum said, "There's Glo and Salim! Oh, Kat, Ted! Ted, *look* at them—remember, look them in the eye—and if Aunt Glo wants to hug you, let her."

"Hrumm," I said.

Then a woman came whirling toward us like a hurricane. That was the only way that I could be sure that she was Aunt Glo, because everything else about her was new. Her black hair was pulled up on top of her head in a new style, a little knot, and she was wearing a pale green dress the color of mint ice cream. Her toenails in new sandals were painted shiny green too, which made me feel unwell. "TED!" she shrieked, and I stepped back and looked up at the white beams of the ceiling.

Then Kat let out a squeal and threw herself at a very tall boy with brown skin who was standing apart from Aunt Gloria. He still looked the same, and he was wearing a shirt I remembered him wearing in May—this was Salim. He grinned at me and held out his hand. "Ted the theoretical joker!" he said. This made me happy because Salim had called me this last spring. He had remembered.

"Hello, Salim," I said politely.

Salim opened his mouth to say something more to me, but then Kat grabbed hold of his arm and pulled him round to her. I could tell Kat was happy to be near him, and Salim was happy to be near her. They were so happy that they were now both ignoring me. And noticing that made me feel as lost and far away from them as the white beams on the airport ceiling.

5

THE ODYSSEY, PART TWO

Then everything went very fast. That was how things moved in New York, Aunt Gloria told us all, over her shoulder, as she rushed us to a yellow taxi that was big enough to fit five of us inside and smelled strongly of cigarettes. We raced down the motorway (it was called a *freeway*, shouted Aunt Gloria—everything in the USA seemed to have a different name, which made me worry that I had forgotten how to speak English while we were flying) and rushed across a huge iron bridge, honking and dodging all the other yellow taxis, which were also in a rush. The sun was burning in the sky (I thought of Helios and his chariot again), and the air was very still.

Kat and Salim were talking very quickly and quietly, and both of them were ignoring me. My throat felt full.

My school shirt stuck to my skin, and my collar itched my neck. My hand flapped. Everyone else was oohing over the sights, but I kept staring down at my gray knees. They have not changed since May. I have grown, but only half an inch. Our yard still takes twelve and a half steps to cross. Usually these thoughts make me happy, but now they didn't. I wasn't sure whether I would fit into New York.

Then the taxi stopped.

I looked up, craning my neck out of the taxi window. We were in front of a tall red-brick building with a staircase on the outside. We went inside, into a lift, which Americans call an *elevator,* that clanked. My suitcase hurt my arm. Kat would not stop wriggling. The sharp corner of her backpack hit my arm. Then Aunt Gloria opened a door, waved her hand and said, *"Voilà!" Voilà* is French for *Here it is!* but Aunt Gloria isn't French, so I don't know why she said that.

I looked through the door and discovered that an *apartment* means a flat. This flat was very small, with wooden floors, and the living room and the kitchen were squeezed into one small space. Three walls of the space were painted white, but one was still brick. I wondered if the builders hadn't finished it. Everything else, apart from the bricks and the floor, was very white. The sofa was white, and even the paintings on the walls were in shades of white. All the books, and what Mum calls *knickknacks,* were missing from the living-room side of the room, and the kitchen side of the room was just a white strip of cupboards and a long white table. I wondered if Aunt Gloria had forgotten to bring the things from her house in England. Or perhaps there was not room for them. That made me worried that there would not be enough room for us.

"Our dear little apartment! It isn't much, but I hope you'll be happy here," said Aunt Gloria.

Salim rolled his eyes and grinned at Kat.

"It *isn't* much," I agreed with Aunt Gloria.

"Ted!" said Mum. "He didn't mean that, Glo."

Aunt Gloria laughed and said that she was quite used to me by now. That made me cross, because she had *told* us that it wasn't much. She had not given any warning that she was using a figure of speech.

I looked around the rest of the apartment and saw that my worry had been right. The whole space wasn't even half the size of our house. I could cross it in only eight steps. There were only two rooms apart from the bathroom and the living-room-that-was-also-the-kitchen. This meant that we had to share, and it was even worse than the time when Aunt Gloria and Salim had come to stay with us. Mum would be sharing Aunt Gloria's room, Kat would have Salim's, and Salim and I would be on futons in the white living room–kitchen. This seemed very unfair to me, because Kat is one person, and there are two of me and Salim. But I thought about how I felt about Kat-and-Salim, and how I missed Salim-and-Ted, and decided that perhaps the arrangement would be good after all. It would give me time with just Salim.

That was the afternoon of August 8. The rest of that day was a blur, because of jet lag. I fell asleep sitting on the sofa while Aunt Gloria and Mum talked, and then again at dinner. So did Kat, although she pretended she hadn't. I kept my special weather watch on British Summer Time so that I could think about the weather at home, and when I woke up in the middle of the night from a dream where I was Odysseus, lost at sea, I could tell that even though it was dark in New York, 1:07 a.m., it was 6:07 a.m. and getting light in London.

There were two people whispering—Kat and Salim.

Kat must have crept out of her room and into the living room. I kept very still and quiet and listened to them.

"I'm so glad you're here!" whispered Salim. "I've missed you! I can't wait to show you the city. You'll love it. Mum's got you all subway passes for the week, so we can go anywhere."

"New York!" sighed Kat. "It's so much better than London! I can already tell."

I was *indignant*, which means upset, because nowhere is better than London.

"Seriously," said Salim. "Though I can't stop Mum hovering over me. She still thinks that—well, the spring might happen again."

Salim, like most people, uses words in a very imprecise way. Of course the spring would happen again. It happens every year as the earth goes round the sun. But I translated what he said into what he meant: Aunt Gloria was worried about him going missing again because of the time he had gone missing before, in London in May.

"And I told you about Mum and Dad!" hissed Kat. *Hissed* is a word that is like *whispered*, but more angry, and it is a good word for the way Kat sounded when she talked about them. "They're being so stupid. I keep hoping I can get Auntie Glo to change Mum's mind."

"Yeah! And maybe Aunt Fai can tell Mum to calm down about me," whispered Salim. "We'll work together, right?"

"Right!" whispered Kat. "We're a team."

I heard Kat getting up to creep back to her room and tried to breathe very quietly. My deductions had been correct: Kat and Salim had definitely been communicating. They were friends, working together—and there was no room for me. Just like in my dream, I was as alone as Odysseus, floating on the wreckage of my ship, all my crew members drowned.

6

ACTING UP

On Thursday, August 9, Aunt Gloria took us to the Guggenheim. She led us out of the apartment and down in the lift, putting her earrings on crooked and smearing lipstick over her mouth as we descended, telling us that the Guggenheim was closed to ordinary tourists that day, because it was Thursday. But she wanted to take us to see it, as a *special private viewing* (her words). She was helping with a new exhibition of paintings that was opening next week—the very first one that she had curated for the Guggenheim. For the rest of the time we were in New York, Aunt Gloria would not be working at the Guggenheim, so she could take us around the city and look after us. She was very excited about that, but I was disappointed. I had wanted to spend all my time in the Guggenheim so I could explore all the patterns there that my encyclopedia had told me about.

I watched Kat and Salim again. They bent their heads close together as they talked, taking the same-size steps. My teacher Mr. Shepherd told me that when you are friends with someone, you mirror their movements and stay close to them, so I could confirm that this morning they were still definitely friends.

Outside, New York felt even more confusing than it had yesterday. The buildings were taller than in London, and they all had stairs on the outside. Everything seemed back to front, and even the people spoke differently. A man in a gray jacket, with dark glasses over his eyes, passed us on the pavement and said, "Morning, guys!" He spoke through his nose, and when Aunt Gloria said "Good morning!" back, I noticed that the tone of her voice had changed to be like the man's. It made me uncomfortable, and my hand flapped. Aunt Gloria was different this summer, just like Kat.

I think Mum must have seen how I was feeling, because she put out her hand toward me, then put it back on her bag again and said, "Ted. Look up."

I looked up and realized that the New York weather was moving in a pattern I could understand. That morning it was in a system of high pressure, with high cirrus clouds. The rising temperature was making my school shirt stick to the back of my neck, just the way it had the afternoon before. I imagined the air above us being twisted into a cyclone by the earth's rotation. This is called the Coriolis effect. It behaves the same everywhere in the Northern Hemisphere (which contains both London and New York). I thought about that similarity, and I was happier.

Aunt Gloria hurried us through the hot square streets, which were too full of people and cars and whirling noise, until a wall of green appeared in front of us. It was a forest, with paths under the trees and lots of people in tight bright-colored outfits, cycling and jogging. There were five different breeds of dogs and seven babies in pushchairs, and my nose was full of the smell of grass as well as gasoline. I made myself think through what I had seen in my encyclopedia, and I realized that we must be looking at Central Park. Central Park was opened in 1876, and it is 843 acres large, which is almost 3.5 million square meters. It has a zoo, twenty-nine sculptures and seven bodies of water. It is even more famous than the Guggenheim.

"Isn't it lovely?" cried Aunt Gloria. "And such a beautiful day! It's like it knew you were coming!"

She was wrong. The weather is not sentient—which means conscious or aware—and so it does not care about people.

Aunt Gloria was fanning herself, and Mum was panting. The sun was very hot now, and an area of high pressure sat above us like a thumb pressing down. My school blazer made my neck and arms itch. The sidewalks were hot and white. We turned down Fifth Avenue, which ran parallel to the park, and I saw that wide blue banners on the streetlights read RICHARD POUSETTE-DART, OPENING AUGUST 17. I recognized this name, and realized this must be the new exhibition that Aunt Gloria was working on.

The pedestrian crossing in front of us signaled DO NOT WALK in bright orange stripes, but Aunt Gloria hurried us forward into the road anyway. There was a scream of tires to our left, and a yellow taxi pulled to a stop, its driver leaning out of the window to shout at us. I felt Mum's muscles go hard under her skin, and she said to Aunt Gloria, "Glo! You might have got us all killed!"

"Oh, Fai, I'm sorry!" Aunt Gloria panted. Her green toenails were squeezing themselves out of her very tight high shoes. The shoes looked painful to walk in. Perhaps that was why she had not noticed the taxi.

Salim snorted air out of his nose. When I turned to look at him, his eyes were rolling. "Mum!" he said to me. "She never looks where she's going. She's the one who needs to be looked after, not me."

"Hmm," I said. I didn't know what to say to this Salim, who enjoyed New York and was friends with Kat, but not with me.

Salim wrinkled his forehead at me. "Hey, Ted?" he said. "Are you OK? I mean—you've been acting strange since we got here."

I wanted to tell him that this was not true. I had been acting exactly the same as always and it was everyone else who was acting strangely.

Salim said, "Listen. I know why you're upset. When I first arrived, I hated it too, Ted. I really did. But I got used to it, and now I think it's great. You'll get used to it too, I promise."

"Get used to it?" I repeated.

"Yeah!" said Salim. His mouth was turning up in a smile. "I love it now. And—listen, all you've gotta do is copy someone who looks like they know what they're doing. That's the way to fit in anywhere—that's how I fit in here. Just act."

"Act?" I asked.

I looked at Salim. His shoulders were back and his feet were apart, and one of his thumbs was stuck through the loop in his jeans. I didn't have a belt loop, so I held my thumb out in front of my hip. I shuffled my feet apart and raised my neck to make my shoulders go down.

Salim showed more of his teeth as he laughed. "Take your hand down, Ted, it looks like it's floating. But other than that, good."

I was pleased. Salim and I had talked, and it had been a good talk. As we walked down the street, parallel to Central Park, I copied Salim. My feet took big strides, and my arms swung. Then Kat wrapped her arm round Salim's and dragged him away from me, talking loudly. But there had been a moment when Salim had remembered how to be Salim-and-Ted again, and I held on to that thought in my head.

7

CRACKS

Then Aunt Glo pointed down the hot white street and said, "There! There it is!"

I looked ahead and saw the Guggenheim. But it was not the Guggenheim I had expected. Its round white outside was covered in scaffolding, sticking out from its surface in ugly lines. There was a man climbing on the scaffolding, in a yellow hard hat and orange coveralls.

"It's being repaired!" Aunt Gloria called to us. "Didn't I tell you? The facade is cracking, so it needs repainting. The builders are doing a wonderful job, but it is a little inconvenient. They broke a pane in the skylight a few days ago! Luckily, it should all be finished by the time the exhibition starts next week."

I looked at the blue caps at the end of the scaffolding spokes. One was loose, and I wanted someone to put it on straight again. My chest suddenly felt tight. The Guggenheim had not been covered in scaffolding in my encyclopedia. It was smooth, clean and white. But this Guggenheim, like Aunt Gloria, Salim and Kat, had changed.

As we came closer to the main entrance, I heard more and more noise. There were people in front of the Guggenheim, taking photographs and talking. I jerked back to make sure they didn't touch me, and my head went to the side. I saw a tourist woman with a camera round her neck and a pink T-shirt that was too tight for her. I saw an old man wearing a brown coat, even though the day was hot. I saw a girl, younger than me, with athletic shoes that lit up on the heels. These people were not allowed in. There was a barrier in front of the entrance, but the barrier was not for us.

"It's such an exciting opportunity!" Aunt Gloria was saying to Mum, very fast, as my feet stepped over the smooth circles on the ground outside the museum. "My first exhibition!" she continued. "It's an honor. I hope

I can do Solomon Guggenheim proud. Now come this way—this door isn't usually open unless the museum is, but I asked for it specially!"

I was wondering how she knew whether Solomon Guggenheim, who was the man who had paid for the museum, would be proud or not, since he was dead and couldn't explain anything, but then she pushed on the front of the spinning glass door and it spun us inside. Even more noise hit me all at once.

On the ground in front of me was an enormous shiny medal that read LET EACH MAN EXERCISE THE ART HE KNOWS. That made me worried. I know the universe, but I don't know any art. I also do not like exercising. I hoped that this was another figure of speech. We walked over it, past a tall, round faced black man in a navy-blue uniform who smiled and winked at us and waved us on, and out into a huge, round, bright white room. I stared up at it. This was the main gallery of the Guggenheim Museum.

I saw what I already knew from my encyclopedia: there were circles everywhere inside the Guggenheim. The main gallery we were in was round. There was a wide curved ramp that started in front of me and curled round the sides of the big circular rotunda gallery six times, making six floors.

This ramp is the most special thing about the Guggenheim. It has smooth stone floors and smooth white sides. It curves upward at a steady three-degree gradient, so it is not hard to walk up. When you are going up or down it, the half wall on your left is low, even for someone my height. Beyond it you can always see the circle of the Guggenheim floor, and the ramp on the other side. This means that you can look across at the other side of the museum and see all the paintings hanging on it on all the levels at once. This is important, and this is what makes the Guggenheim so special. Here you can see things differently and look at them together, up and down as well as next to each other.

On the right of the ramp, the wall tilts slightly outward, and that is where the paintings are hung. There is lighting that climbs upward with the ramp, protected by a long triangle of glass that is translucent rather than transparent. When it's turned on, it gives out a soft yellow light, but that morning the lights on the second and third floors were off.

The ramp circled all the way to a huge round window at the top, ninety-six feet above the ground. I squinted up and I could see the broken windowpane Aunt Gloria had mentioned, a place where the color of the sky was brighter.

On my left, across the circle-patterned stone floor of the Guggenheim, was a set of triangular white stairs and a shiny metal lift. I knew that the lift and the stairs went all the way up the six levels of the building, like the ramp. Next to the stairs, on each level, were smaller side galleries and rooms in the tower building, separate from the main one, where other paintings and sculptures were displayed.

This was all correct, and exactly how I had imagined it. But what was wrong was everything else.

There were ten tall, thin wooden packing crates stacked on the floor near where I was standing, so I couldn't see any of the circle patterns properly. I could smell paint. A stocky white man in overalls, with big shoulders and a wide freckly face, was standing next to the bottom of the ramp, holding a hammer. On the first level, above us, a woman with dark hair tied back behind her ears was sawing through a piece of wood. She looked like my science teacher Mrs. Huang, so I thought she might be Chinese. A short white woman with red hair walked in front of us up the ramp with some thin plywood boards, and the Chinese woman shouted at her not to drop any. A skinny young black man walked past the Chinese woman, head and shoulders low, and vanished up the curve of the ramp. Ten seconds later, a drill began whirring. Two curves of the ramp up from him, another man was working, but I couldn't see him properly. There was a hoover vacuuming somewhere above us, and it mixed up with the drill noise and the people shouting at each other.

My hand shook itself out, and I could feel my head going sideways. "Hrumm," I said. *"Hrummmmm."*

Mum put her hand on my arm. "It's all right, Ted," she said.

But she was wrong.

8

WAYS OF SEEING

"This will all be gone in time for the opening, of course!" Aunt Gloria called through the banging and whining and buzzing. Every noise echoed around the Guggenheim, just like someone blowing into a shell. "Our special maintenance crew have taken down the old paintings and put them in their boxes, and once they have finished repainting the ramp and altering the space, they'll get out the new paintings and hang them up. I've been very particular about where each one goes. It'll look so lovely! Fai, have I told you how the Guggenheim is altered for each new exhibition? Sometimes they even add in false walls for the paintings to hang from. It's so clever."

Mum whispered in my ear, "Breathe, Ted. Stay calm."

I thought about Odysseus on his ship. That calmed me, so when a man came up to us and said, "Ms. McCloud!" I could look across at him. I wondered who he meant, and then remembered that Mum's name before she married Dad was Faith McCloud, and so Aunt Gloria's name would be McCloud too. I realized that this was the tall black man who had waved us through the revolving door. He was the security guard, and he was finally coming to make sure that we were secure.

"Good morning, Lionel!" said Aunt Gloria. Her voice had gone high and nasal again. "I hope it's all going well?"

"Absolutely, Ms. McCloud," said Lionel, showing all his teeth. "No problems here. Salim, what's happening?"

"Lionel!" said Salim. He was smiling—he was happy to see Lionel. "This is my aunt Faith and my cousins Ted and Kat Spark. Remember I told you about them? Sparks, this is Lionel. He's one of the security guys here. He's brilliant."

I looked at Lionel, who had a round stomach as well as a round face, and very short dark hair. He was smiling, calm and casual. He winked at me. I wondered how good

Lionel was at being a security guard. He seemed very friendly, and he smiled all the time.

"So this is the Guggenheim," said Salim to Kat and me, nodding around at it. "I thought it'd be really boring at first. But I've actually realized that it's cool. It's way better than Mum's last job, anyway. Do you want to see some paintings? The tower gallery on the second floor's still got paintings, even though the rotunda is empty. Lionel, am I OK to take them up?"

"Go crazy," said Lionel, grinning at Salim again. "Your mom told us she'd be here by this time, so you're all expected. Just don't knock anything off the walls, all right?"

Lionel had made a joke. So Salim and Lionel were friends too.

We did not go into the lift to get up to the tower gallery—we went up the steps themselves, two sets of nine of them, turning through two sets of sixty degrees, with small triangular lights set into the walls. Then we were facing the huge white ramp of the Guggenheim again, one level up.

To our right there was a doorway, and when we stepped through it, we were suddenly in a rectangular room with white walls and a low ceiling. The tower galleries are shaped like normal museum rooms, but they have hidden layers that made them much more interesting than they seemed at first. At the other end of the room from the doorway, the wall was only half as high as it should be, and light came up from below and above it. All the tower rooms in the Guggenheim are connected by a space that you can stare down into or up at, depending on where you are. Below us was the gift shop and above us was the tower gallery on the third floor.

Then I noticed the paintings on the gallery walls. On my right was a painting that was a rush of greens and oranges and blacks, bursting left and right and up and down. There was no pattern to it. Next I looked at a painting that was just scribbles and dots on white. I thought it looked like Morse code, but I couldn't read it. Then I found myself staring across at a painting where a green woman floated in a red sky.

"It looks like a dream!" said Mum.

I did not agree. I do not dream like that.

On the wall opposite the green woman, just underneath a square white security camera, was a painting that looked like it had been framed twice—first in a thin white square and then, inside that, in a lopsided black border of paint. It made the rest of the painting look tilted, off center, with red and black and yellow lines and shapes shooting in all directions.

"That's by a man named Vasily Kandinsky," said Salim. "It's called *In the Black Square*. You should like it, Ted. It's all about the weather."

I looked back at the painting. It did not look like the weather at all. It looked like chaos.

"It is!" insisted Salim. "Look, that's a rainbow, and those are clouds, and that's the sun."

"How do you know that?" asked Kat, blinking at him.

"Hey, I pretend not to listen to Mum, but I do pick some things up," said Salim. He glanced at Aunt Gloria, and she raised her hands and pursed her lips.

"My boy!" she said. "Fai, what can I do with him?"

I stared at the picture again, and this time I imagined that I was not looking at a sky, but the *code* for a sky, like the way when you are drawing a circuit diagram in science, a lightbulb becomes just a circle with a curved line through it. If those lines in the painting were like isobars in a weather forecast, and those circles were all the places the sun is in one afternoon, laid out on the same space, like a time-lapse photograph . . . I suddenly saw it.

And I liked the picture very much.

9

PROTONS, ELECTRONS AND NEUTRONS

Then another woman came hurrying into the gallery. She was white, about the same age as Aunt Gloria, and her blond hair was pulled back neatly in a bun on her narrow, neat head. She was very small and slim, and she wore a tight blue skirt, a white shirt and high-heeled blue shoes. She was carrying a big handbag, which she shifted around on her shoulder.

"Gloria!" she said. "Not the Kandinskys again!"

"I love them, Sandra," said Aunt Gloria, laughing. "I can't help it—I know you don't feel the same way! Sandra, this is my wonderful sister, Faith, and her kids, Kat and Ted. I've told you all about them and their visit.

They're my lifelines, truly they are. I'm so lucky they are here."

Aunt Gloria often exaggerates. I saw Mum's mouth purse at *wonderful,* and her eyebrows go up. But then her mouth went up in a smile and she put her arm round Aunt Gloria. "We are so happy to be here," she said. "And what a lovely museum this is!"

"It is very special," said Sandra, her mouth going up too. "I'm so pleased to meet you. The whole museum heard you'd be coming today. I'm Sandra Cook. I'm—"

"My assistant curator!" cried Aunt Gloria. "My *other* lifeline, ever since I arrived here. I don't know what I would have done without her! Sandra's been here for five years, and what she doesn't know about this museum . . ."

She didn't finish her sentence, and I wondered what it was that Sandra didn't know.

Dad would have explained, I thought, and I wanted him there. With only Mum, things felt out of balance, changed. Inside an atom there are electrons, protons and neutrons. Remove one of the protons and the atom becomes something different, a new element. If my family were all parts of an atom (this is a metaphor, and I was proud I'd worked it out), then Kat, Aunt Gloria and

Salim were definitely electrons, spiky and unpredictable and flying in circles, and Mum and Dad were sensible protons. I decided that I was a neutron, which has no electric charge at all. These are only there to give the nucleus of the atom mass, and so sometimes scientists do not notice them until they are gone.

Would this mean that Kat and Salim would only properly notice me if I wasn't there? I glanced over at where they were standing together, whispering and laughing. Then I checked my weather watch to see what time it was in London. It was 3:21 p.m., which meant that here it was 10:21 a.m. I felt better.

Then I realized that I was not hearing the conversation happening around me. Sandra and Aunt Gloria and Mum were still talking. "She's been such a help to me as I've navigated the first few months of this wonderful opportunity," said Aunt Gloria. "Really, Fai, I feel like this is finally where I'm supposed to be. They take me seriously here, and this art—it's simply priceless. Salim likes it too."

Salim sighed.

"Salim!" said Aunt Gloria. "You know you've taken to the Guggenheim. You know everyone and you're here almost every day. Quite a favorite, my Salim."

"I'm here almost every day because ever since what happened in London, whenever I'm not at school, you won't let me out of your sight!" said Salim. His mouth was twisted as though he was joking, but his arms were folded. It was as though the two parts of his body were saying different things. I deduced from what he was saying now, and what I had overheard last night, that Salim was not happy that Aunt Gloria was worrying about him so much.

Then my nose began tickling. I smelled something strong, and it made me cough. I turned toward the doorway we had all come through. I walked toward it, and my eyes stung as well. It was like I had felt the time when I had been in the garden and Kat had dropped a cigarette behind the garden shed. It had caught fire and burned a tall scorch mark on the shed wall before Dad put it out.

"Mum!" I said urgently. "Mum! I think something's on fire!"

10

FIRE, FIRE!

"Don't be silly, Ted!" said Mum. "It's just— Oh!"

Suddenly a new noise went shrilling through the air. It was very high and loud, and it made my hand shake itself out so hard that it hit Kat. She yelled and hit me back. I glared at her.

"Oh good Lord!" cried Aunt Gloria. She rushed us out of the tower gallery and back into the main rotunda, and I saw that thick white smoke was billowing up toward us from the first floor, filling the round main space of the Guggenheim.

"Fire!" gasped Aunt Gloria. "Oh Lord, not today, not *now*! Faith, take the children outside, quickly. Sandra, help them! Go out through the front door. It's quickest! I need to stay and send everyone else out that way—I'm a fire marshal, I have to make sure they're all safe."

Sandra rushed us down the ramp to the first floor, through the thick cloud of smoke, and then motioned us out of the spinning door that we had walked through earlier. "Go on!" she said. "Go and wait outside on Fifth Avenue. I have to go back for the others!"

Mum's hands were grabbing hold of me, her nails scratching my neck. I wriggled, but she ignored me. We ran out of the main door, coughing and rubbing our eyes. A crowd of tourists was gathering, talking and pointing at the smoke. It was very thick now, and even though the spinning door was glass, I could not see anyone inside.

I looked at Salim and saw that his eyes were wide and his mouth was very thin.

"Is Auntie Glo going to be all right?" Kat asked.

"Of course she is," said Mum, but her lips were thin too. "She just has to make sure everyone else is all right. Salim, Kat, stay here and don't worry."

We watched the doors. Then they spun open, and the people who had been working in the museum began to come out, coughing like we had been. I saw the stocky, freckled white man from the maintenance crew, along with another man I had not seen before. He was medium height, and he had brown skin and lots of dark curly hair on his head and face. He was wearing a dark blue Guggenheim uniform. Then I saw the red-haired woman. Sandra came to the doorway and ushered out the skinny black boy, who I now saw was not much older than Salim and had his hair cut in a big square around his thin head, and then an old black man. This man was very short and small, with a small white beard, and his eyes were crinkled up in his wrinkly face. The Chinese woman with the ponytail followed him, striding along, her wide mouth twisted up and her nose wrinkled, and then Lionel, who was not smiling anymore either.

The red-haired woman was running when she came outside, her pink cheeks puffing out, and so was the old man, but Lionel and the boy and the Chinese woman moved slowly. I thought that they must be telling their bodies to act calmly, and I was impressed. They all gathered around us.

Sandra was standing just outside the door, her blond hair coming out of its bun. Lionel the security guard was shouting something into a mobile phone. Everyone's arms and bodies were very close. I could also hear sirens coming from behind me and to my right, and the alarm was still going.

Smoke, thick and white, poured out of the Guggenheim's main door every time it spun open, and I realized that in a few minutes I might see the fire. I imagined it like a tongue, licking at the inside of the building. This made me think about all the atoms of wood and paint turning into atoms of charcoal in the fire. It seems like a magic trick, but it's only chemistry.

"Thank heavens there aren't more people in there!" gasped Mum, watching the smoke. "Though—goodness, think of all those paintings!"

"But they're priceless, Mum," I said sensibly.

"*Priceless* means expensive, you neek," said Kat.

That was very Mean Kat of her—*neek* is what some people at my school call me. It is a cross between *nerd* and *geek*, but worse than both. Then I felt angry at people who do not use words in a scientific way. How could *priceless* mean exactly the opposite of itself?

Salim's face twisted up, and he said, "Aunt Faith, Mum's all right, isn't she?"

"Of course she will be," said Mum. "She'll be out in a moment."

But I was worried that she was telling a lie.

11

NO SMOKE WITHOUT...?

Just then, Aunt Gloria burst out of the smoke that was filling the main entrance to the Guggenheim. I glanced down at my weather watch. It was 10:28, exactly seven minutes after the alarm had sounded and we had left the museum. Her mouth was open and her eyes were wide, and she was wearing a bright orange vest over her dress. "Everyone is out!" she gasped. "Oh, what a disaster!"

"Calm down, Gloria," said Sandra, putting her hand on Aunt Gloria's shoulder. "It's time for you to do the roll call."

I knew that this was an American phrase that means the same as *taking the register.*

Then I noticed that the Chinese woman was standing with her hands on her hips, as though she wanted to be in control. Her ponytail swung, and her eyes were narrowed. She had a square chin and broad shoulders.

"I've checked my crew already," she said to Sandra. "All of us are here."

"Gloria still needs to do a full roll call," said Sandra. Her lips went very thin and she put her hands on her hips too. I saw that her nails were long and shiny. "It's the rules. Go on, Gloria."

She handed Aunt Gloria a clipboard, and Aunt Gloria began to read out names. I discovered that the ponytailed woman in charge of the maintenance team was called Helen Wu, and the other woman, the redhead, was called Lana Juster. The muscly man with freckles was Ben Katz, the young skinny man with the square hair was Ty Green, and Jacob Teller was the old man with the white beard and wrinkles. The man with lots of curly hair who had come out with Ben was called Rafael Rodriguez. I deduced that he must have been the person using the hoover earlier, so he was a cleaner.

Everyone standing outside had answered the roll call. But then Aunt Gloria called out, "GABRIEL GARCIA!" and there was a gap in the noise.

"*Gabriel?*" she shouted again. "Has anyone seen Gabriel? He's not still up on the scaffolding, is he? Oh Lord—"

"He's there!" said Helen sharply.

I looked and saw a tall muscular man with a wide face and brown skin like Rafael's coming round the curve of the museum. He was wearing orange coveralls undone to the waist and holding a yellow helmet in one hand. With his other hand he was rubbing his face and yawning. I realized this was the man I had seen climbing on the scaffolding when I first arrived at the museum.

"Gabriel!" said Aunt Gloria, gasping. "Thank goodness. Oh Lord. At least everyone is all right! But, oh God, the paintings!"

The sirens I had heard were getting closer. The smoke inside the museum door was very bad, and I pictured the fire eating away at the inside walls. I wondered why I still had not seen any flames.

"The fire engine's coming!" said Mum to Aunt Gloria. "They'll save them, Glo!"

"I pray it's not too late!" said Aunt Gloria dramatically.

Then the fire crew did arrive, in a huge red truck with a screaming alarm. Four people got out of it in a rush, all wrapped up in gray-and-yellow-striped suits and heavy helmets, and went thumping into the building. I looked at my weather watch. It was now 10:32 a.m. in New York.

Inside the building the fire alarm stopped.

Five minutes passed according to my weather watch before the four people in the fire crew came back out. One took off his helmet and said something to Aunt Gloria, and Aunt Gloria's face dropped open. She turned and came staggering back over to us as though someone had clobbered her.

"Fai," she whispered. "The fire—there isn't one. It's just *smoke*. They found a smoke bomb in the first-floor stairwell, and another in the rotunda gallery, at the bottom of the ramp."

Mum stared at her. "So—was it some kind of prank?"

Aunt Gloria shook her head. "I don't know. At least—at least the paintings will be all right." Then she burst into tears. I thought it was odd that she was suddenly more upset than she had been, now that she knew the paintings were safe.

Mum looked at her, and then at us. "Salim," she said. "Can you look after Ted and Kat for a while? Go across the road and into the park. I need to stay here with Glo."

"Fai, Salim can't go on his own!" said Aunt Gloria.

"Of course he can," said Mum. "He's fourteen, isn't he? Glo, remember that he can look after himself. But, Salim, don't you move from where I've told you to go, do you understand? Stay where you can see us."

Salim nodded at her. His face was a strange mix of emotions that I could not read. And I suddenly had a bad thought. Salim was a practical joker. What if Kat and Salim had been planning this joke? Could they have set off the smoke bombs?

12

THE PHENOMENON OF SPONTANEOUS COMBUSTION

We crossed the street into Central Park and stood under the leafy green trees—in New York, I thought, it was easy to go from the city to the country and back again in a few steps.

We were on a rectangle of grass under one big tree, with a path to our left and the edge of the park on our right, and six trees with thick bushes beneath them in a row blocking us from the road. I could just see a slice of the Guggenheim and its scaffolding between the bushes and the sky. I drew lines from us to the path, and from us to the trees, to triangulate us in space, and that made me feel good. I wiped the whole of New York out of my brain, so that there was only the park, and us, and the sky.

"Can you believe that about the smoke bombs?" said Kat, her eyes wide. "Who do you think did it?"

Was Kat being truthful, or was she only pretending not to know? I stared at her, trying to work it out.

Then Kat narrowed her eyes. "Salim," she said. "*You* didn't—"

"Hey, it wasn't me!" said Salim. "I like a joke but I'd never do anything that dangerous, all right? Setting off smoke bombs—they cost serious money, and they might do serious damage. And Mum would go spare."

I looked at Salim's face. He was staring straight at Kat, his hands held up. I have read that people who are lying look away from the person they are talking to, and fold their arms, so I thought that the balance of probability was that he was telling the truth. I remembered what had happened in the Guggenheim. Salim had been with us since we had arrived, and I had not seen him setting off any smoke bombs. That was good. I was very glad that my suspicion had been incorrect. Salim was not guilty, and so neither was Kat.

"So, do you think . . . ," Kat began. Then she stopped.

I have noticed that lately Kat has begun to stop sentences halfway through, like an adult. "I mean, who—"

"Hey!" said Salim. "It's Ty!"

The boy from the Guggenheim was coming toward us, out of the bushes. He was walking a bit stiffly and he was wearing the blue jumpsuit that all the crew had, undone to his waist, with a white T-shirt showing under it. His head jerked upward when he heard Salim call his name. His face was thin, his eyes were large and his mouth was flat, not smiling.

I took a careful step backward. There are older boys at school who laugh at me—the ones who call me a neek— and this boy looked tall and strong enough to be one of those. His shoulders and his eyes said that he was not afraid of anything, and his big square haircut was definitely cool. I tried to stand like Salim had shown me, upright and open, but my hand shook itself out and I couldn't stop it.

Then Salim said, "Hey, Ty!" and stepped toward him, not away. I remembered what Aunt Gloria had said—that Salim knew everyone at the Guggenheim. So Salim and this boy, Ty, were friends.

"My man Salim!" said Ty, and his mouth smiled and

he held out his hands. He stepped onto the grass where we were. "What are you doing here? Where's your mom?"

"Very funny," said Salim, although his face did not look as though anything was funny at all. "Aunt Fai got Mum to let us go off on our own for once, while they check the museum."

"Yeah, that's why I'm here too," said Ty. "We have to keep out while Lionel's doing a sweep to make sure there's no damage."

"Ty's the coolest member of the maintenance crew," said Salim to Kat. "It's always great when something electrical breaks, and he can come round."

Ty smiled at Salim, and now that I knew that Ty was not a bully like the boys at my school, I could breathe deeply again. Kat and Salim and Ty flopped onto the green grass, and Salim put his hands behind his head to hold it up.

"Sit down with us, Ted!" said Kat.

I shook my head. Standing felt safer, because I wasn't sure whether Kat and Salim really wanted me there. But then Kat and Salim and Ty began to talk about the smoke in the museum, and I listened, because I was also interested in it.

Before I had heard about the smoke bombs, I wondered whether I had finally witnessed spontaneous combustion. Spontaneous combustion is an Unexplained Phenomenon, like the Bermuda Triangle. I am fascinated by Unexplained Phenomena, and when I grow up, as well as being a meteorologist, I would like to solve some of them. When Salim disappeared, one of our possible theories was spontaneous combustion. It didn't turn out to be true, which was good but also sad because it meant that I was no closer to understanding what it was. It was a very complicated feeling.

Now that I knew about the smoke bombs, and also that Salim had not set them off, and that there had been no actual fire, I was sad because once again I hadn't witnessed spontaneous combustion, but also interested because this explanation left many questions unanswered. For example, who *had* let off the smoke bombs, and for what reason?

"But why would anyone do it?" asked Kat. "It must have been a joke, right?"

"What a joke!" said Ty, raising his shoulders. "If the smoke's stained the walls, *we're* gonna be smoked. We'll have to paint everything again. Look, Salim, be real with me: You didn't have anything to do with it, did you?"

I thought that this proved to me that Ty did know Salim well—he knew that he was a practical joker.

"No!" said Salim. "Why does everyone keep saying that? You know Mum'd kill me."

"Well, *someone* did it," Kat pointed out. She was squinting, and I could tell that she was thinking. "Salim," she said after a pause. "We need ice cream."

13

AMBITIONS AND SINKHOLES

That was not what I had been hoping for. The conversation had just begun to get interesting. But I do like ice cream, so I agreed.

We went to a cart across the path—it meant stepping outside my triangulated area, which was not good, but the cart had the same Magnum ice cream that I always get in London, and that was good. When I get a Magnum, I like to zip open the plastic wrapper and then crack off and put aside the chocolate outside before I can eat any of the vanilla middle. I imagine that I'm pulling away the surface of the earth in perfect sections, tectonic plate by tectonic plate, and underneath is the smooth vanilla-flavored magma core. I like the fact that even though a Magnum is one ice cream, it is chocolate on the outside and vanilla on the inside, as though it is two versions of itself at once. It changes, but actually it is still the same.

"I've never seen anyone do that before," said Ty. "That's cracked!"

"Ted's weird," said Kat, biting into the rainbow sprinkles of her cone.

"Hey, Kat, Ted's cool," said Salim.

I gave Kat my best glare. She usually eats the chocolate plates once I have finished with them, but she was not getting them this time. I offered them to Salim instead, because he had said I was cool, but he shook his head *no*.

"Can I have them?" asked Ty.

I looked at him. He had called me *cracked*. But Ty's mouth was smiling, and he was holding out his hand without touching me. I thought about it, and then I realized that although *cracked* was a word that means insane, it was also a word that was a good and accurate description of what I had done to the Magnum. I also realized that Ty had used the word on purpose, because he knew that. He was someone who played with words, a theoretical joker, just like me.

"You're a crack ice cream demolisher. You should be a professional!" said Ty. He was showing me that I was right in my deductions. I saw why Salim was glad to be his friend.

"My dad demolishes buildings," I said. People don't usually think that Dad and I are similar, but what Ty had said made me realize that in one way, at least, we are. As a reward, I held out the chocolate casing to Ty. He balanced it on his palm, and before it melted, he built it into a new shape, a sort of domed bridge. I liked that. I decided that Ty had a good brain.

"When I get older, I want to do the opposite," said Ty. "Design buildings, not break them. Maintenance crew's just for now. I'm saving money to enroll in a course, and one day I'm going to be an architect." Then, when his sentence had come to an end, he pushed the whole chocolate bridge into his mouth at once. Kat laughed, and so did Salim.

"So, what about you?" Ty said to Kat.

Kat's brows pulled together and her arms folded. "What *about* me?" she repeated.

"I want to design buildings," Ty said. "Salim wants to be an actor as well as a photographer—right, Salim?"

Salim nodded.

"So what about you?" Ty asked Kat.

Kat paused. Then she said, "I want to be a fashion designer."

People in stories, especially in myths, never change. In the book *The Odyssey*, no matter what happens, Odysseus is always clever and arrogant (which means rude), and Athena is always wise. This is very reassuring to me.

But in real life people are not like that. They change all the time, faster than I can ever learn about them. I knew that Salim liked to act and take pictures, but Kat had never said anything to me about being a fashion designer. I had never thought of Kat wanting to be something. Kat is just my sister. That is who she is. Then I thought about the way she had been behaving that summer, and I started turning facts into new conclusions in my head:

1. *Fact:* Kat hates history, and math and science, and wants to do art and design GCSEs. *Old conclusion:* She prefers smoking

behind the bike sheds to lessons, and so wants to do GCSEs that would let her do that. *New conclusion:* She really likes art and design, the way I like science and history.

2. *Fact:* Kat has been driving Mum and Dad spare (Mum's word) about her GCSEs. *Old conclusion:* She is being Mad, Mean Kat. *New conclusion:* She actually cares which GCSEs she takes, because she has an ambition.

3. *Fact:* Kat gets angry when Dad teases her about her fur-collared jacket, or her haircuts, or her painted nails. *Old conclusion:* Kat is angry at Dad in general. *New conclusion:* Kat is very interested in clothes and hair and nails.

Final conclusion: Kat is telling the truth. She wants to be a fashion designer.

There are things called *sinkholes,* which can open up without warning in the street, or even in someone's house. You don't know they're there before they appear, but then they do, and beneath them there can be miles and miles of empty space, ready to suck everything down into them. That was how my final conclusion made me feel. There was a cavern opening up in the Kat I knew, a sinkhole that changed the shape of her forever.

"Really? Cool," said Ty. "How do you become one of those?"

"You make your parents let you study art and design," said Kat, sticking out her bottom lip. "And then you have to make a portfolio, and do internships. But to be chosen for the best internships, and the best design schools, you have to have money, or you have to get discovered."

I frowned because I could see Kat standing in front of me.

"Hey," said Ty, nudging her. "I found you! There you go, you've been discovered."

Salim laughed. I decided that I definitely liked Ty.

Kat's mouth wrinkled. "Not like that," she said. "You know. *Discovered.* By a fashion designer. They need to see me and see how interested in fashion I am so they'll hire me as their intern and pay for me to go to design school and I won't have to live in stupid south London with my stupid *parents* until I'm old, studying math and science and becoming a nurse like Mum."

"Kat's really good at designing!" added Salim. "She's been sending me pictures of what she's been working on."

Salim's face and body were pleased, but I was upset. "What she's been working on," I repeated.

All three of them turned to look at me.

"Oh, Ted, don't make that duck face!" said Kat. "I couldn't tell you—I couldn't tell Mum and Dad. They'd just say that I wasn't being serious."

I was angry, because I would not have said that to Kat. If her drawings were good, I would have told her they were good. *This* was what Kat and Salim had been emailing about. They had kept me out of the secret of Kat's ambition.

So I decided that I could do something without Kat or Salim, right there and then. I made a list in my head of the possible perpetrators of the smoke-bomb trick:

1. A tourist had crept past Lionel and set off the smoke bombs. This was unlikely. Lionel had been standing by the entrance to the museum, watching who came in and out.

2. The smoke bombs were set by someone who worked at the Guggenheim. I tried hard to remember all the names I had heard at the roll call earlier—Lionel, Aunt Gloria, Sandra, Rafael or one of the five members

of the maintenance crew: Helen, Ty, Lana, Jacob and Ben. This was very possible.

3. The smoke bombs were set off by Gabriel the builder. This was more likely than the tourist theory, but less likely than it being one of the people inside the museum, because Gabriel had been working on the *outside* of the museum, on the scaffolding. I thought that he could still have thrown the smoke bombs inside the museum through the broken pane of glass in the skylight, but they would have made a loud noise when they landed on the floor, which someone would probably have heard.

4. The smoke bombs weren't smoke bombs at all, but examples of spontaneous combustion. I already knew this was not true, but it was still a good thought.

I stared back across the road at the bit of the Guggenheim I could see. Perspective made it look very small.

Ty's phone beeped and he flicked it open. His eyebrows went up. "Something's happened," he said. "Come on—we need to go back!"

He turned back to the Guggenheim and began to move toward it quickly. Kat and Salim followed him, and so did I. My body copied Ty's, not Salim's, because I was still angry with Salim. I noticed that Ty was moving less stiffly than he had before. He was worried.

When we stepped back through the spinning main door of the Guggenheim, people were running up and down the ramp, and they were all shouting.

"What's going on?" Salim asked Lionel, who was standing by the entrance, yelling into his walkie-talkie.

"I just saw it," said Lionel. He was not smiling now. His face was creased up and he was sweating. "In the tower gallery. One of the Kandinskys has been stolen!"

14

THE DEFINITION OF TRAGEDY

Aunt Gloria would not stop crying. Mum and Sandra and Kat and Salim all stood around her holding things out as she sat on the main floor of the Guggenheim: tissues and glasses of water, and a slice of cake that Salim brought her from the café. Lionel was calling the police, and Helen Wu was talking to the rest of the crew in a low voice. I wanted to hear what she was saying to them, but Aunt Gloria's crying was too loud.

Aunt Gloria buried her face in a handful of tissues (I thought that was very wasteful of her, considering the environment), and waved away the water and cake. "Not—" she gasped. "No—my diet!"

"Not for me either, thank you, I'm gluten-intolerant," said Sandra, so Salim ate the cake.

"Glo, love, come on now," said Mum, patting her shoulder. "The police will be here soon, and you need to talk to them."

Aunt Gloria sobbed some more and waved her hands about in the air. "I'm the most senior staff member here!" she wailed, and the sound made me wince. "The director will be furious! He's in Beijing this week—not even in the country. What if—what if—he blames me? What if he wants someone's—someone's—head on a plate?"

I imagined someone's head on a plate, and deduced that Aunt Gloria was using a figure of speech. But I still didn't know what she meant.

"Glo, don't be silly," said Mum, sounding very firm. "Come on, sit up! *You* didn't steal it, did you? *You* didn't set off the smoke bombs! So it isn't your fault that it's gone. It's terribly sad that it's missing, but it's just a painting. *You're* quite all right, and so is everyone else—no one's been hurt."

Aunt Gloria sniffed and dabbed at her eyes with a tissue. "I suppose so," she said. "But, Fai. That painting! It's so beautiful—and it's been stolen! This is a *tragedy*."

Aunt Gloria was exaggerating again, I knew. A *tragedy*

is a disaster or a cataclysm. When Odysseus's ship is sunk in *The Odyssey* and everyone else drowns, it is a tragedy. When Salim went missing in the spring, we thought it might be a tragedy. That was frightening. But I did not think that a missing painting was the same thing at all.

Salim had explained to us that the painting that was missing was *In the Black Square*—the tilted, black-bordered painting by Kandinsky we had seen in the side gallery of the museum earlier, the one Salim had told me was about the weather. I thought about its bright red and yellow circles and triangles with black lines running through them, Kandinsky's code for the weather, and I thought how strange it was that we had seen it on the wall of the tower gallery less than an hour ago. It had been right in front of us, and now it was gone. It was like the x of an equation that had not been solved. That was very interesting, but it didn't seem important enough for someone to cry over. I told Aunt Gloria so.

"Ted!" cried Mum.

"The police will find it," I said. "It's very large, and so it will be difficult to hide."

"Ted!" said Aunt Gloria. "You don't understand. When a piece of art is stolen, it's very hard to find it again. Only five percent of all stolen art is ever recovered."

I was impressed that Aunt Gloria knew a fact like that. "Why?" I asked, but Mum said that this was not the time.

"And what if it *is* never found!" gasped Aunt Gloria. "What a loss that will be!"

Then she started to cry again.

The police came. Blue-and-white police cars screeched up the road, and officers stretched fluttering blue-and-white tape across the entrance of the Guggenheim. We all had to leave the museum so that they could do a full search, so we stood on the hot street outside while the police checked all the way through the building to see if the painting was hidden somewhere inside. They went up the ramp and into all the tower galleries.

But they could not find it.

Then a policeman came to talk to us. I found out that he was not a normal policeman, but a special art detective. He was a black man about Dad's age, with short dark hair, gold-rimmed glasses and a long brown coat, like detectives have in films. He was very serious, and his mouth was always in a frown. He asked if we had seen anything. Kat and Salim said no. I started to tell him about the ten boxes, and the five people in the maintenance crew, and Rafael who had been hoovering, and Gabriel on the scaffolding, but the detective seemed more interested in talking to Mum.

I thought this was stupid. The detective who had helped get Salim back when he went missing in the spring had wanted to know everything. I thought it was good that it was only a painting that had gone missing this time, not a person.

The detective wrote down what Mum said in a small leather notebook, and then he told her to take me and Kat and Salim away while everyone who had been working in the Guggenheim was interviewed. I thought this was even more unfair. I wanted to stay. I wanted to know more about the theft. But the detective shook his head and waved us away.

I turned back to watch him as he went inside the Guggenheim. His arms and legs were very long, and they all moved at slightly different rates, as though he had not calculated how the different parts of his body fitted together. I understood that. The detective was a bit like me—but also not like me at all, because I am good at noticing things, and I make sure to pay attention to everything.

15

FIVE PERCENT PROBABILITY

It was almost dark by the time Aunt Gloria arrived back at the apartment. We ate Chinese food that Mum had ordered out of white cardboard boxes, because Aunt Gloria was too upset to cook. I stared into my box of food and felt a bad feeling creep up my esophagus. It did not look like the sweet-and-sour chicken from Golden Mountain, the Chinese takeaway on the corner of our road. I took a bite and it did not taste like the sweet-and-sour chicken from Golden Mountain either. It tasted bright orange, like tinned tangerines. I put it down, and decided that I did not like traveling at all. There were too many strange things, and they all made me feel exactly like Odysseus, alone on the sea without his crew: very small, and very lost.

"It's really gone," said Aunt Gloria in a shaky voice. "Taken out of the gallery. The police found out that the security camera and burglar-alarm systems were cut earlier today, so the robbery must have been planned in advance. The traffic cameras at the end of the street show a moving van driving away from the Guggenheim at exactly the right time this morning. The police are trying to trace it now."

"So perhaps it *will* be part of the five percent!" said Mum. "And we can go back to enjoying our holiday."

I was impressed that Mum had remembered Aunt Gloria's fact, but I wasn't sure I believed her. What had happened might not be a tragedy, but it was a very big thing that would change everything and everyone around it.

"Yeah," said Salim. "And maybe, Mum, it would be OK if Kat and Ted and I could go and see some sights on our own?"

Salim had said *and Ted*. I looked at him to see whether he was pretending or not. He winked at me, and I understood that he wanted me to say something.

"Hrumm," I said. "Yes, I want to see Times Square."

This was true. According to my encyclopedia, Times Square was very interesting.

"Absolutely not!" said Aunt Gloria, ignoring me and still talking to Salim. "Ted might get lost. And you're still new to this city, Salim. It's not safe."

"Yes it is!" said Salim. "It's just as safe as anywhere. Mum, you've got to get over it—I've told you that the London Eye won't happen again!"

Aunt Gloria *erupted*. This is a figure of speech that does not mean that lava burst out of the top of her head, but her face turned red and her mouth opened wide and she shouted, "I thought you were *dead*, Salim! I can't just *get over it*!"

"Glo, Salim's learned his lesson, surely," said Mum. "You shouldn't coddle him."

"Don't you start, Fai," said Aunt Glo, still red. "What about *your* daughter? She knows what *she* wants to do, but *you* won't let her do it."

"That's because she's far too young to make such a silly decision about her future!" Mum said, flushing red just like Aunt Gloria.

"Fai, don't you remember how I was at Kat's age?" asked Aunt Gloria. "I knew what I wanted, just like she does, but our mum would never see it. Don't you make the same mistake."

"Mistake?" said Mum. "Glo, you were unemployed for *years*! The worries I've had over you . . ."

And just like that, the evening turned into a loud argument that made me feel hot and messy inside.

I walked to the side of the living room and tried to call Dad at home, but he didn't answer. The line clicked and purred, and then I heard our answering machine message start. I imagined the sound traveling all the way from Rivington Street, through the telephone lines and the cable under the Atlantic Ocean, to my ear. Then I remembered that Dad wasn't answering because it was 2:16 a.m. in London. That made him feel further away than ever.

I put the telephone down and went to Salim's room, where Kat was staying.

I got up on Salim's narrow bed, which was blue, white and orange, with the word METS in curly letters on the duvet, and hit the wall, the way I do at home. I knew that Mum would be angry with me, but the feeling built and built in my head until I groaned and thumped his pillow, again and again, making it a pattern. *Thump THUMP thump, thump THUMP thump.*

That felt good. I could think again. Sometimes, when I want to shake my hand out, or groan, and I know I can't, I get that built-up feeling in my head. It wraps itself around everything, like a low-lying mist, until I can't tell where I am, or what I'm thinking, just the way someone stuck in a mist doesn't know which way they are going, or where they have been. People lost in the mist can sometimes go round and round in circles, just a few meters from their house. That is how I felt.

I lay back on Salim's bed and thought about the whorls of the Guggenheim, about the circles on its floor. I thought that if I owned somewhere like that, I would not put anything in it, or let in any other people. I would just sit in it and feel everything moving around me in a pattern. That would be perfect. But real life is just as messy as Aunt Gloria and Mum's argument, and in real life people had got in, and one of them had stolen *In the Black Square*.

The shouting outside had stopped.

I opened Salim's door eight centimeters and heard Mum and Aunt Gloria talking in lower voices.

"You know that we love you, Glo," said Mum.

"Of course I do!" said Aunt Gloria. "Oh, Fai, I am lucky to have you as a sister!"

So the argument was over, and they were friends again.

I got off Salim's bed and went to brush my teeth.

Brushing your teeth is important. If you don't do it, you are at higher risk from tooth decay and also gum disease. I stood in Aunt Gloria and Salim's bathroom, making sure to brush each tooth, inside and out. The light over the mirror was greenish, not yellow like ours at home. It made me look different. I stared at myself.

Was New York Ted the same Ted I had been in London? Was all the change around me making me change as well?

16

WAKE-UP CALL

The next morning I woke up to the sound of the phone in the apartment ringing. After the sixth ring it stopped. Then it started again.

I sat up very carefully so as not to wake Salim, who was asleep on the futon next to me. Aunt Gloria had fallen asleep at the kitchen table, an empty glass of wine next to her hand. Mum had told us not to disturb her last night.

On the sixth ring Aunt Gloria's eyes opened, and she snatched the phone just in time.

The phone squawked like Kat when she is arguing with Mum, and then a soft chatter came out of the end of it into Aunt Gloria's ear. I watched her face and saw it lift, her eyes widen and then her mouth open, wider and wider, until I could see not only Aunt Gloria's incisors and canines, but all the way back to her molars. The second from the back on the left-hand side had a silver filling in it. I have heard Mum say that Aunt Gloria has a *sweet tooth,* so I suppose that must have been it.

Aunt Gloria's tongue bobbed, and her mouth closed and opened and closed again. The phone whispered into her ear, and then it stopped. Aunt Gloria said, "No. Yes. I see," which is the least I have ever heard her say. I deduced that whatever the phone was saying was very bad. Then she put the phone down.

There was a noise from the door that led to the bedrooms—Mum was awake too, and she was standing there in her blue nightie with the hole in the collar. Kat was with her, yawning and looking cross.

"What is it?" Mum asked. "Glo, love, what's wrong?"

"The police," whispered Aunt Gloria. Her face was a very pale color. "They've traced a moving company that apparently picked up a crate they think contained the painting. The moving people didn't have anything to do with planning the robbery—they were just hired to take a packing crate from the back of the Guggenheim to their warehouse. And they were hired by someone who said they were *me*. They gave *my* credit-card details for the van and . . . and for buying smoke bombs, and they used a Guggenheim computer and telephone to do it! Oh, Lord!"

"Glo, what on earth!" cried Mum. "You *didn't* have anything to do with it, did you?"

"*No!*" gasped Aunt Gloria. "Of course not! Someone must have . . . have stolen my credit-card number, and used my computer when I was out of the office. But— Fai. The police are coming here. They want to take me in for questioning. I think they want to *arrest* me. What will I *do?*"

"Glo!" said Mum. "They'll realize soon that you *couldn't* have stolen the painting, even if your card was used. You were with us all the time yesterday morning!"

Then I saw Mum's face sag as she remembered a fact that I already knew: Aunt Gloria had *not* been with us the whole time. She had been the last person to leave the Guggenheim before the fire crew arrived.

"They're going to try and blame me!" gasped Aunt Gloria. "They're going to put me in prison!"

"Mum!" said Salim. He was sitting up on his futon, and his face was creased with worry. "Mum, are you serious?"

"They're coming here now," said Aunt Gloria, whose face had gone a strange grayish color. "I can't let you see them arrest me! I can't—I can't— *Oh!*"

"Mum!" said Salim again. "Calm down. It'll be OK, I promise. I'll help you."

I didn't know how he could promise that. I felt frightened. Aunt Gloria was going to be arrested. My head went to the side and my hand shook itself out.

"Salim!" Aunt Glo gasped. "My wonderful boy. I know you will. Oh, what I wouldn't do for a cigarette!"

"Glo!" said Mum, her mouth in a tight line. "Don't let this lead you to take up smoking again, *please*. But I think we could both use some coffee. Salim, go downstairs to the coffee shop and get your mum and me coffees." She paused. "Take your time—get yourself something to eat too. All right?"

"Of course," said Salim. "Don't worry, Aunt Fai."

Mum was trying to show Aunt Gloria that Salim was responsible, I thought, and also get him out of the apartment so she could talk to Aunt Gloria.

"I'll go with him," said Kat, as quick as lightning. I am

using a figure of speech again. Lightning typically takes two milliseconds to strike the earth, so it is not actually true that Kat moved that quickly, but she spoke very fast, her eyes flickering from Mum to Aunt Gloria and back again.

"Thank you, Kat," said Mum. "And—take Ted with you too."

"Mum!" wailed Kat. "Not Ted! Come on!"

This was what I was expecting. I felt sad. It was still Kat-and-Salim, and that hurt me. But then I looked at Kat and saw her close one eye at me. Why was Kat winking at me?

"Either Ted goes too or no one does," said Mum. "Choose, missy."

"Fine," growled Kat, so mean that if my memory was not so good, I might have thought I had imagined the wink. "Ted can come too."

Kat went to her room to change. When she came back, she was wearing a long belted shirt with sparkles on it, tight jeans, and long feathers in her ears, like a bird. I thought it looked stupid, but then I remembered that it was fashion, and Kat wanted to be discovered.

"Kat!" cried Mum. "You can't go out looking like that!"

"Mum, honestly, I'm fourteen!" said Kat, her face

going stiff and turning away to the side in exactly the way she teases me about.

"Exactly!" cried Mum. "You're not old enough."

"Your mum has a point, Kat. Do you know how many girls like you get kidnapped every year in New York?" asked Aunt Gloria, wiping her eyes.

"No," said Kat. "Do you?"

Aunt Gloria opened her mouth and then closed it again, and expressions chased themselves across her face like clouds in a localized gale.

"That is not the point," she said at last.

"Come on, Mum," said Salim. "We're only going to the coffee shop!"

Aunt Gloria put out her hands as though she was trying to catch hold of him across the room. But she only reached the edge of his shadow, and as I could have told her, shadows are only the effect of light in front of an object, not a real thing. You can't touch one any more than you can actually sit on clouds. That only happens in myths. "Come back soon," she said quietly. "I can't bear to lose you again."

"Muuuum!" groaned Salim. "Come on!"

Aunt Gloria's eyes went moist again. "You'll always

be my baby boy," she whispered. "Just like Kat is Fai's little girl. Oh, go on, get out."

We stood in the lift while it went down six floors, and then we walked out into the street. The sun was already hot, but there was shade under the trees. I looked around at the bright, tall, tan-colored buildings with their exposed fire escapes, inside out like beetle exoskeletons. New York felt very different from London.

"Kat," I said. "You winked at me."

"Of course I did," she said. "Ted, something awful's happened."

"I know," I said. "Aunt Gloria's about to be arrested."

"Detective Ted!" said Kat. "Yes, she is. The painting's been stolen, so the police need to blame someone. Aunt Gloria makes sense. Her credit card was used, she *was* the last person in the Guggenheim yesterday morning, and the police will think that all that crying she's been doing is suspicious. But *we* know that she didn't do it."

Some of what she was saying was true, but some was just guesswork. And it still did not explain the wink. I stared at her.

"Ted, can you stop looking at me like that?" snapped Kat. "You've been so *weird* since we arrived. You've barely talked to us. Anyone'd think you didn't like us anymore. So, are you in?"

I blinked.

"In where?" I asked.

"Aunt Gloria's about to be arrested," Kat said. "The police think it's her, so we can't trust them. But who do we know who solved a mystery that even the police couldn't? Who do we know who are detectives?"

"Detectives," I said, because I did not believe that Kat was really saying what my ears were hearing.

"*Us*, you idiot," said Kat. "The two of *us*—I mean, mostly you. And that means we can do it again, right? We can find out who really stole that painting. And stop doing that repeating thing, otherwise you can't help."

"So, *are* you in?" asked Salim. "Will you help solve the mystery?"

"I am probably in," I said. "Let me think about it."

Kat smiled. "*Probably* means yes!" she said. "I know it, Ted!"

"Hrumm," I said.

17

$X + Y = ?$

We stopped off at the corner shop to get our breakfast, as well as Aunt Gloria's and Mum's coffees. Salim and Kat's idea of breakfast was sweets and fizzy drinks (which Salim said was called *soda* in New York). I didn't have any sweets, because they all looked very different and I was worried about E-numbers. Then I realized that the *E* in E-number stands for *Europe*, and we were not in Europe anymore. So there were no E-numbers in these sweets, only food additives. Even chemicals had different names in the USA.

I breathed slowly in and out three times—once for me, once for Salim and once for Kat—and then asked for a Coke, but I wasn't sure about it when the shopkeeper handed it to me: it was in a tall, thin glass bottle instead of a fat red can, and it tasted at least twice as sweet and very sticky. I held it out in front of me and watched a drop of water crawl down its side. The water flashed in a rainbow, which meant that it had caught the white light from the sun and refracted it out into all its hidden colors. At least the laws of physics did not change in different countries.

We sat down on a bench outside the shop. I still didn't think I understood the mystery properly. I was also worried about detecting in New York.

"What's wrong?" asked Kat, jerking her head at me.

"*Why* does it matter who really stole the painting?" I asked.

"Ted!" said Kat. "Come on!"

"*Why?*" I repeated. It was all I could say.

"Because *Mum* matters," said Salim. "She loves her job, and if she goes to prison, she'll lose it. And she likes it here. I know she's still worried about me after the spring, and I wish she'd let me have a bit more freedom—but if I help work out who stole the painting, that might help her see that she can trust me. And I love it here now too. At my new school, no one calls me . . .

that horrible name I told you about in the spring. I'm still a drama geek, but that's kind of cool here. What Ty said—about me wanting to be an actor—I'm going to try out for *Cat on a Hot Tin Roof* this fall, I mean autumn, and after I'm done with high school, I want to go to drama school here."

I remembered Salim as the boy who had not bent back his New York guidebook once before coming to this city, and Kat as the girl who slipped out of school to smoke, and who argued with Mum. But this Salim was happy in New York, and this Kat was a grown-up Kat, who knew what she wanted to be. I thought of Dad saying, "My little kitten!" and I wondered what he would think of her now.

"You *can* solve the mystery, Ted," said Salim. "You and Kat worked out what happened to me, after all."

"Yes, we did," I said. "We worked through all the possible solutions until we arrived at the truth."

"Yeah," said Salim, his expression changing to happiness. "You did. The police couldn't, but you did. And you can do it again."

My hand flapped. "I don't know," I said. "I know I said I could, but . . . I don't understand New York."

"Yeah, but you understand *problems*," said Kat.

"I don't understand *people*," I said. "I don't understand you and Salim. Why were you talking to each other
and not me? Why didn't you tell me you wanted to be a
fashion designer? Are you still my friends?"

"Ted!" said Salim. "What? Why would you think we
weren't friends anymore? Kat only asked me not to tell
you because—"

"Because I knew you'd tell Mum and Dad," said Kat.
"And you'd do it in that stupid Ted way that'd make them
side with you and tell me off. It always happens, and it's
not fair!"

She sounded angry, but when I looked at her, I saw
that her mouth was shaking and her eyes were wet.

"Ted," she said. "I was stupid, and I'm sorry I've been
cross with you. It's just—look, it's not easy, being part of
your family. You don't know it, but you need so much.
All the time. Appointments and lessons and—*things*,
Ted. And the more things you have, the less there is
to go around. And I know you don't mean it, and you
can't help it, but sometimes I wish . . . I wish everything
wasn't always about you, all right? When I try to make
it about me, I get yelled at. Mum and Dad want me to be
sensible all the time, but I *can't*."

"I can't help being me either, Kat," I said.

"I know," said Kat, wiping her eyes. "And being you is a good thing to be. It really is. Because when something like this happens, you can help solve it. I *know* you can."

"So can you!" I said, because it is true that Kat made some very clever deductions during our last case.

My mind was spinning. *Could* I do it? When Salim went missing, I'd had the tube and the phone book. I had been at home in London, but all the same I hadn't been able to see the real pattern until it was almost too late. Could I do it again, in New York, where everything was the wrong way round? I imagined the words *Who stole the painting* as an equation. The painting was x, just the way I had imagined before. The thief was y. But there were several different variables on the other side. First, we were in New York, not London. Also, Salim would be with me, not just Kat. Salim and Kat were both different than how they had been in May, so even though they told me they were still my friends, I couldn't be really sure how they would behave. My hand shook itself out, because I wanted to go back to our house, and our garden, and Dad. New York + Ted + Salim + Kat = $x + y$ was a difficult equation. It didn't balance, like London + Ted + Kat − Salim = Salim + x, where x marked Salim's spot.

But then I remembered that, just like the earthquake

in America that had caused the tidal wave in Japan, London and New York were connected. That meant they had things in common, patterns that I could find. No matter how strange this mystery felt, I knew I could turn it around into something that I could solve. When Salim went missing, I learned that this is how my brain works—this is what makes me special and different, and different is not a bad thing.

And when I thought that, I knew that even though it gave me a bad feeling all the way up my esophagus, I had to help Kat, and I had to help Salim and Aunt Gloria. We were family, and now I had discovered that we really *were* also friends.

I also knew what I had to say, the secret password that would make Kat happy again. "Kat," I said. "*Sis.* I think I can help solve the mystery."

Kat squealed. "All right!" she said. "And we've also got Salim this time. We'll be unstoppable!"

"Yeah!" said Salim. He put out his hand, and Kat put hers on top of it. They both waited. Then Kat giggled.

"Bro," she said. "You're supposed to put your hand on top."

"No thank you," I said politely.

18

THIRTEEN SUSPECTS

"We have to start with what happened," said Kat in the tone of voice that Mum always calls *bossy*, jumping up from the bench where we were sitting and walking back and forth in front of me and Salim. She went in and out of the shade from the shop's green awning, turning bright in the sun and then darker in its shadow, again and again. "Someone set off smoke bombs, the smoke alarm went off, everyone ran out of the museum and, when they came back, the painting had been stolen. It was put into one of the packing crates we saw on the first floor, then taken to the back door of the museum and picked up by a moving company we know was hired using Auntie Glo's credit card."

I thought carefully about what she had said. It seemed simple, but it was really not simple at all.

I considered the smoke bombs first. We knew about them because the firefighters had told Aunt Gloria, and she had told us. This is called *anecdotal evidence,* and it means any evidence that a detective hears about. In this case, because the firefighters had said it, and they are generally trustworthy, it was probably still useful information, but anecdotal evidence is really the weakest kind of evidence there is, because it is only based on what someone says, and as I have discovered, most people are better at lying than I am.

The smoke itself, though, was different. We could *prove* that it had been there, because we had seen it with our eyes. This is called *empirical evidence,* and it is better than anecdotal evidence. But although it seems like good evidence, it is still not the best kind, because (as Kat and I discovered last time) your eyes can trick you. The best kind of evidence is *scientific evidence*—evidence that has been tested and proved to be correct. As far as I could tell, we didn't have any scientific evidence yet.

Then I thought about everyone running out of the museum. Mum, Salim, Kat and I had got out very quickly, but the rest of the museum staff didn't all come out at the same time. They had appeared one by one, apart from Ben and Rafael, who came outside together. It had been seven minutes before the last person, Aunt Gloria, had appeared.

Then, four minutes later, the fire department arrived, and they were in the building, unsupervised, for five more minutes.

I said all this to Kat, and she narrowed her eyes. I was worried, until I decided that this look was her thoughtful narrowed-eyes look, not her angry one.

"We need to write this down," she said. "Salim, do you have something to write with?"

Salim pulled a piece of paper and a pen out of his pocket, and with his help, we made a list of all the people we had seen leave the museum:

IN WHAT ORDER DID PEOPLE LEAVE THE GUGGENHEIM?

1. Ted, Kat, Salim and Mum (Aunt Faith) left the building at 10:23 (two minutes after the alarm first went off).

2. The freckly man from the maintenance crew

(Ben) and the man with lots of curly hair
(Rafael, who Salim says is the janitor) left
together at 10:24.

3. Lana, the short woman with red hair, left just
   after Rafael and Ben, at 10:24.

4. Sandra, blond and slim, was standing at the
   doorway of the Guggenheim from 10:25.

5. Ty, Salim's friend, who is skinny with a big square
   hairdo, left at 10:25.

6. Jacob, the old man with a white beard, left just
   after Ty, also at 10:25.

7. Helen, the woman with a ponytail who is in
   charge of the maintenance crew, left at 10:26.

8. Lionel, the tall security guard, left at 10:27.

9. Aunt Gloria left the building at 10:28, seven
   minutes after the first alarm, and five minutes
   after Ted, Kat, Salim and Mum.

10. The builder, Gabriel, was working on the outside
    of the building, and we don't think he ever went
    inside. But he was late for the roll call, which is
    suspicious.

11. The firefighters arrived four minutes after Aunt
    Gloria left the Guggenheim, at 10:32, and came
    out five minutes after that.

Looking at this list, I was worried. There were so many suspects.

"Would the first people out of the museum have had enough time to steal the painting?" asked Salim. "Rafael and Ben only came out a minute after us, and Lana came out just after them."

We did not know how long it would take to steal *In the Black Square* yet, but I agreed with Salim that it would be more difficult for people who only had two or three minutes to do it. We could not rule them out yet, but they were not as good suspects as the people who had come out later.

"Also, the thief would have to be strong, wouldn't they?" asked Kat. "The painting's big, and it's probably heavy."

"It is ninety-seven point five centimeters by ninety-three point three centimeters," I agreed. I had looked it up on Salim's computer.

"It's in a wooden frame too. And those packing cases are also very heavy," said Salim. "I tried to lift one once! There's no way that Mum could manage it, or Sandra either."

"Definitely not Sandra. She's really small and slim. *And* she was wearing Manolo Blahniks," said Kat, nodding.

I frowned at her.

"They're *shoes,*" Kat said, sighing. "Really expensive designer shoes. The gorgeous high heels Sandra was wearing. Remember? I don't think Sandra could have lifted anything in them."

"Right, that's one point against Mum or Sandra," said Salim. "And also against Ben, Rafael and Lana, because the timing is trickier. Now we have to work out how to rule out Mum properly. Hey! I know. If we can prove Mum wasn't the one using her credit card to order the van, then we can prove she had nothing to do with the theft, and someone else stole it from her bag and used it! So all we need to do is find out which moving company it was and go and see them. They might be able to tell us when the card was used. Maybe it was a day when Mum wasn't even in the office. Or maybe the person who placed the order didn't sound like her."

I did not think it was right for Salim to say *all we need to do* like that. I thought that Salim was expecting this to be very simple and easy, but I was not. The police were far ahead of us in this investigation. They had found the moving van by looking at traffic cameras—traffic cameras that we didn't have access to, the way we'd had access to the film in Salim's camera when we investigated our last mystery. Salim had a new camera now, a digital one, but even a digital camera couldn't show us all the things the police could see. The police had discovered which moving company the van was from. They would already be following that lead.

But Salim was smiling. "Listen, we don't need cameras to work out where the van came from. We've got something just as good. We've got Billy."

"Billy?" I asked.

"Billy's—well, you'll see," said Salim. "He'll help us find the moving company. Then we'll be able to prove it wasn't Mum easily! All we have to do is go back to the Guggenheim."

"How are we supposed to do that?" asked Kat, raising her eyebrows.

"We'll tell Mum and Aunt Fai that we'll be all right while"—Salim swallowed suddenly in the middle of his sentence—"while they're answering the police's questions. We'll say that we're going to . . . sightsee. All right?"

"Hmmm," said Kat. "All right. Ted, can you lie, if Mum or Auntie Glo asks?"

"Just copy me, Ted," said Salim, nudging me. "Just do exactly what I do and you'll be fine."

"I'll be fine," I repeated.

But as we walked back to Aunt Gloria's apartment, I had a nervous feeling in my stomach. I was about to tell the fourth lie of my life.

19

RED AND WHITE AND BLUE, PART ONE

When we got back, though, we found that Aunt Gloria's apartment building was lit up not only by the bright white sun, but also by flashing lights, red and white and blue. Red, white and blue are the colors of both the British and the American flags, and also of the American police, and that was what these lights meant: the police were here for Aunt Gloria.

"Oh no!" said Kat. She and Salim began to run, and I chased after them as quickly as I could.

There were two police cars flashing their lights, and one other car that was gray, with a Connecticut license plate. I recognized this car from the Guggenheim the day before: it belonged to the art detective. I had a bad feeling, because seeing that car made Aunt Gloria being arrested go from a possibility to a high probability. And when we opened the door to Aunt Gloria's apartment, that probability became a certainty.

The art detective was in Aunt Gloria's living room. He was still wearing his long brown coat, even though he was inside. "You have the right to remain silent, of course, but anything you say can and will be used in evidence against you in a court of law," he was saying to Aunt Gloria, leaning over her threateningly and glaring at her through his gold-rimmed glasses.

A lump rose up my throat, because I knew from Mum's TV shows that this was the thing you say to someone when you are arresting them.

Then he turned and saw Salim. "This must be your son," he said, frowning.

"Salim," said Aunt Gloria. She was dressed, and had made up her face, but her mascara was running. I deduced from this that she had been crying. "My boy. You shouldn't be here, you shouldn't be seeing this." She turned to Mum, who was standing next to her, looking very worried. "Fai, help me, please, you have to come with me to the station, please. . . ."

Aunt Gloria was not using her *right to remain silent*. I wanted to point this out to her. I nudged Mum, but she said, "Not now, Ted. Glo, you know I'm coming with you. It'll be all right. I'll be there. You go downstairs with Lieutenant Leigh, and I'll be right behind you. Now, Salim, Kat, Ted, listen to me."

Aunt Gloria was being led out of the door by the detective. He moved awkwardly, as though his left leg did not know what his right leg was doing. I was watching him, and Mum had to take my arm to turn me toward her. "I'm going to go with Gloria," she said to us. "It will all be OK, I *promise*, but I don't know how long we will be. So Glo has called Sandra, and she'll be here soon. She's going to look after you. You have to stay with her, and be good, until we're back. Do you all hear me? Ted, are you listening? Do you promise to wait here for Sandra?"

"Yes, Mum," I said.

"Kat, Salim, do you promise?" asked Mum.

"Yes, Mum," said Kat.

"Yes, Aunt Faith," said Salim.

"And, Kat, you'll look after Ted, won't you?" asked Mum.

"*Yes*, Mum!" said Kat.

"Oh," said Mum, and her eyes were suddenly wet.

"I'm sorry about all this. Salim—I'm so sorry. I promise *it will be all right.*"

Then she turned and went out of the door after Aunt Gloria and the detective. The door slammed behind her and we were alone.

Salim's mouth was drawn down and his eyes were small. He was upset. Kat reached out her right hand and patted his arm.

"It'll be all right," she said.

"It *won't*," said Salim. "It's just—it really happened. Mum got *arrested.*"

"Yeah, she did," said Kat. "But that doesn't change anything. We can't just wait for Sandra. We can't change our plan. It's even more important now. Come on. We don't have much time."

She went running into her room and came back with her leopard-skin backpack bulging as though it was about to spill open. I realized that inside it was Salim's new camera and everything else she thought we might need to be detectives in New York—I could see the New York guidebook, a notebook, her tiger-striped pen and three bottles of water—and I was proud of Kat. She still wanted us to detect, and I realized that she was right, and that she was making good decisions. This made me feel safer.

"Ready?" asked Kat.

"Ready," said Salim. "Ted?"

I liked that he was asking me what I thought. And although I knew that Mum and Aunt Gloria would be angry with us for lying to them and not waiting for Sandra, I finally understood how important it was that we solved this mystery. It was worth disobeying the adults for. It was worth stepping out of the apartment into a city I did not know. "I'm ready," I said.

And just like that, we walked out of the apartment again. I was in New York with my lightning-bolt sister and my practical-joker cousin, and we had a mystery to solve.

20

SEEING BILLY

This time we walked to the Guggenheim using side streets. This was so that Sandra wouldn't see us on her way to the apartment. Salim turned off his phone, which meant that Sandra couldn't call us either. It made me feel as if Salim and Kat and I were on an important mission, or possibly even a quest.

I realized, though, that it might be hard to hide in New York. This is because the street names in New York are very sensible. They are set out in a numbered grid that starts at the bottom of Manhattan (Manhattan is the part of New York we were in), and you count upward, both south to north, and east to west. The Guggenheim, for example, is on Fifth Avenue, between Eighty-Eighth and Eighty-Ninth Streets. New York is a city set up for logical people, but this meant that it would be more difficult to move randomly through it and confuse anyone who might be looking for us.

We came out onto Fifth Avenue at Ninetieth Street and stared down it at the Guggenheim. As we moved closer, I saw that there was still police tape all around it. It flapped in the breeze, white and blue, set out in a square, but a lopsided one. There were also two cars parked in front of the Guggenheim's main door—two white-and-blue police cars, to match the police tape.

When we saw those police cars, Kat made a noise and Salim said "Quick!" and pulled Kat and me back off Fifth Avenue onto Eighty-Eighth Street. This was because he didn't want to be caught by them, since we had run away from Sandra.

While we were on Eighty-Eighth Street, across the road from the museum, we were hidden from the police and their cars. I could look at the Guggenheim from a new angle. The curve of the main building was to our right, scribbled all over with scaffolding, and there was a tall tower in front of us. From Fifth Avenue I had seen the Guggenheim as just a white shell shape, but from this side I saw how the tower building, where the painting had been stolen from, was also part of it. The tower had been added onto the back of Frank Lloyd Wright's round building in 1992. This was done because the people who ran the Guggenheim needed more space to work, as well as show paintings. The new tower is made of concrete and it looks just like all the other high buildings around it. It is very ordinary. At the base was the loading bay, where the moving company had collected the packing crate yesterday with—although they had not realized it at the time—the stolen painting hidden inside.

Its doors were closed now, and there was more police tape around the loading area, as well as markings on the ground and small yellow plastic stands with numbers painted on them. I deduced that the police had left these to show where they had found clues.

A woman in a gray suit and sunglasses walked past us, tapping at her phone. She pushed past a man in a gray suit and sunglasses coming the other way and also tapping at his phone. I wondered whether people in this part of New York had a uniform, like I did. That idea made me feel pleased.

Neither of the people looked down at a white man on the ground, sitting between a black iron gate that read

1080 and a black double door that read NATIONAL ACADEMY MUSEUM. He was sitting on a flat piece of cardboard that read UN-MAID R, he had dirty green trousers and a dirty blue shirt with two buttons missing, and his face was covered with a hairy brown beard. There was a notebook in his lap, and he was holding a pencil.

I know from *The Odyssey* that how people look has nothing to do with how important they are. Odysseus dresses up as a beggar so that he can creep back into his house. His enemies do not see him because he doesn't look how they expect a hero to look, and that is how Odysseus finally defeats them. This story is a good reminder that you should notice everyone you meet, especially when you are on a quest.

"Billy!" said Salim, waving at him.

Kat's face scrunched up in a way that I knew meant disgust, because Billy looked and smelled as though he had not washed for a long time, and she hitched her leopard-skin backpack further up her shoulder.

The man grinned up at us. His top left incisor was missing. "It's my friend Salim!" he said. He did not speak very clearly.

At that moment a policeman in a blue uniform came round the side of the Guggenheim. He was looking to his right, at the loading-bay doors, and not to his left, across the road at us.

"Quick!" said Salim, waving his arms. "Down!" He crouched down on the pavement, his arms resting on his knees, and shuffled backward until he was leaning against the black double door next to Billy. Kat copied him, and I did too.

"On the run from the law?" asked Billy. I wondered how he had lost his tooth.

"The usual," said Salim, and he closed one eye at Billy. Salim was winking to show that he was joking with Billy.

"I knew I liked you, Salim," said Billy.

"How's the morning been?" asked Salim.

"Not bad, not bad," said Billy, lifting his shoulders and twisting his face up. "Mostly police plates. Local. Got that Oregon one over there, though, and there was a van from Ohio at nine-fifty-two."

"Billy collects cars—well, mostly he collects their license plates," said Salim to me and Kat.

"Got 'em all in my book!" said Billy, hitting it with his hand. "Got almost all the fifty states. Just waiting on Hawaii."

"Oh!" said Kat, and her mouth made an O as well.

Now I understood why Salim had brought us here.

Billy wrote down the license plates of cars that passed him. He would have written down the license plate of the moving van yesterday, and we could use it to get to the painting.

"What vans do you have in your book from . . ." Salim paused.

"Ten-twenty-one onward, yesterday morning," I said. That had been the moment the alarm went off. I had seen it on my weather watch.

"That's why we keep you around, Ted," said Salim, and he smiled at me. I was pleased.

Billy opened the book and flicked through the pages. Salim raised his camera and took a picture of him while his head was bent, reading. Light and shade fell down across Billy's body and the white page. I saw that it would be a good picture.

"Black Toyota," he said. "Gray Chevrolet. Blue Toyota. White Chrysler. Ram ProMaster. Fire trucks at ten-thirty-two, but they came from downtown and parked off Fifth, so I just heard 'em, didn't see 'em. Wait—ten-thirty-four—here's one. Green van. New York plate: NJK AND. I remember that one particularly—driver got out and loaded up a packing crate from the Guggenheim bay, then drove away again."

I felt my heart speed up in my chest.

"That's it!" hissed Kat. "That's the painting!"

Our theory, and the police's theory, had been partly proved: the moving company *had* taken away a packing crate. We were on the right track.

"Did you notice anything about it—anything on the van?" asked Salim.

Billy narrowed his eyes at his notebook. "Yeah. There was a lightbulb on the side, and it had a funny name. . . . There it is. Effortless Light Moving. That help? What's this about, anyway?"

Salim's mouth stretched into a very wide smile. "Oh," he said. "Just the painting that was stolen yesterday."

"No one tells me anything," said Billy.

We had our first clue.

Salim got up from his crouch to see if the policeman had gone. Then he nodded at us and stood all the way up. While Kat and I stretched, Salim pulled out his mobile phone and turned it on to call directory assistance.

"Hello," he said, his voice very flat and calm even though his face was upset. I watched him, trying to learn how to make my voice lie like that. "Can I have the telephone number and address for Effortless Light Moving?"

I have noticed that New Yorkers do not say *please*. My theory is that they are moving too fast for it, just like those people in business suits were moving too fast to see Billy. That made me worry again about the speed of our investigation. What if we were too slow to solve the mystery in this city?

While I was wondering this, Kat zipped open her backpack and pulled out her pen with tiger stripes and a notebook with pink-and-green flowers. She held them out to Salim, and he took them and wrote, leaning the notebook against Kat's sparkly shoulder as he did so. Then Salim just hung up the phone (no saying *thank you*) and switched it off again so that Sandra could not call us. Then he turned to us, eyes wide.

"They're in Brooklyn," he said. "Water Street."

Kat folded her arms and stuck her chin out. This was the Kat I knew from the mystery of the London Eye, the Kat who had run halfway across London following leads, the Kat who did not let anything stop her. I knew this Kat, and I liked her.

"Right," she said. "Salim, take us to Brooklyn."

21

BROOKLYN WEATHER

To go to Brooklyn, we had to get on the subway.

Here are some things I know about the New York subway. It is more than one hundred years old. The first official subway system opened in 1904, and it never stops. It runs twenty-four hours a day, seven days a week, like an electrical circuit.

I also know that the New York subway map is not like the London tube map. The tube map is topological, which means that it shows the relationships between stations, but not how far apart they really are. You always know how the station you are at connects to all the other stations, and that feels very sensible. But the

New York subway map shows the true space between things.

I had been looking at the subway map before we arrived in New York. I knew that the nearest lines to Aunt Gloria's apartment, and the Guggenheim, were the 4, the 5 and the 6 trains, and the codes for them all are green circles with the numbers inside them (in London, green means the District line). But everything I had learned about the subway still did not prepare me for what it felt like to be in the subway itself.

The London tube is tiled, and the stations where the trains pull in are smooth white parabolic curves that are perfect for holding the red-and-blue curves of the trains. The New York subway is concrete and metal. You can see all its wires, down the tracks into the black tunnels. Everything is shiny, and people's voices echo around in it and make my head hurt. When I saw the station platform, I stepped backward and my head went sideways. My arm began to flap.

"Come on, Ted!" said Kat. "It's not so bad."

I took ten deep breaths. Then the metal turnstile bit down behind me and I was on the platform, just as a train shot into the station, its surface rippling with reflected strip lights. It was very hot, and people were talking. I saw an old man in a baseball hat with his lip hanging down and a stain on his collar. I saw a girl with her hair cut into a bright blue peak like a mountain. She had earbuds in, and she was nodding along to something only she could hear. I saw a woman in high heels running forward with a cup of coffee. A drop splashed on her arm, and she wiped it away. I tried to make the people around me into a pattern so I could cope.

When I finally stepped on the train, I thought about astronauts. I imagined that the silver train was a spaceship, and the blackness around us was as empty as space.

"Hey, Ted," said Salim. "Look. We started at the Eighty-Sixth Street stop, and we're counting downward with the streets. The next one's Fifty-Ninth Street, right, and then Fifty-First. When we get to Bleecker Street, below Fourteenth Street, we change trains."

I knew Salim was trying. I tried too, because we were on a quest. I sat the way he was, with my back against the seat and my legs stretched out, and watched 59 becoming 51 becoming 42 becoming 33. I listened to the rattle of the train's wheels or the hiss of music coming from ten pairs of headphones or the old lady singing to herself in the window seat.

"Ted!" said Salim in my ear. "Time to change trains!"

We crossed the platform, the hard white lights above us flickering.

Then we took the F train (orange, like the Overground in London). This train rattled through three stations and suddenly burst out of the tunnel into bright light. We were on a bridge over a river. The bridge was brown metal and it made diamond patterns against the window as I stared out. It felt like being on Waterloo Bridge, and that was good. I was coping, and I was proud of myself.

But when we stepped off the train, I thought that we had come out in a different city. We were in a construction site surrounded by big gray and brown warehouses. The bridge was above us, stretching back to New York (or forward, into Brooklyn, depending on how you looked at it), and in front of us the road was dirty, covered with torn paper and plastic bags and drinks cans. Even the sky looked more yellow. I knew that this was just an effect of the sun shining through pollution—it was a trick the sky was playing on me—but it still felt bad. Salim raised his camera and took a picture.

"We've come to the wrong place," I whispered to Kat.

"No we haven't," she said. "This is Brooklyn. It's just another part of New York. It's just like being in . . . Stratford, Ted. Or Brixton. Or . . . Ealing Broadway. Before, we were in Manhattan, which is like . . . Russell Square, or Piccadilly Circus. It's still all the same city, like London. Do you see?"

Kat had made a pattern in her head. She had laid out the map of New York and put a map of London on top of it—a topological map, not one that followed real geography. I was impressed. Kat was also seeing the world differently, and if Kat could do it, then so could I.

So I let Salim lead us across the loud, dirty road and down a side street. We passed a yellow sign for a taxi service and a blue sign for a costume rental store and then I saw a green sign with a lightbulb on it that read EFFORTLESS LIGHT MOVING. LITTLE GUYS, BIG PLANS read smaller words under it. That felt like a sign to me. Perhaps the universe was making a pattern after all.

Salim pressed a buzzer. There was silence, a crackle, and then the door opened with a thump.

22

OH, HONEY

We were in a dark stairwell, with seventeen steps leading up to a brown door. It opened and a woman's face peered out. I was suddenly worried again. I remembered that we were somewhere we were not supposed to be, meeting people we did not know anything about. What if she had a gun? Americans always have guns in films.

"Hello?" she called down to us. She saw us, and then all her face appeared, along with her body, wearing a short black dress that was too small for her. She was white, with shiny brown hair and a small straight nose. "Hello!" she said again. "Can I help you?"

Kat nudged Salim. Salim nudged Kat.

"We're here because my aunt is being accused of stealing a painting, which she did not do," I explained. I thought I was being helpful, but then Kat kicked me and hissed, *"Ted!"* I remembered about lying, and that I am not very good at it.

"What do you mean?" asked the woman. She had an expression on her face that I couldn't understand.

"Don't worry about him," said Kat loudly. "He doesn't know what he's talking about. We've been sent by Gloria."

The woman's face changed. She said, "Oh, honey!" She stretched her hands out toward us. "If Gloria sent you, come in."

"Yes, she did," said Salim. "I'm her son and these are my cousins."

The woman said, "Come upstairs, honey. All three of you, come on."

I was not sure if we should follow her—we did not know her, after all—but Kat was stepping forward, and so was Salim. I decided to copy them. This woman was the first test we had to face as part of our quest.

We climbed the stairs, first Kat, then Salim, then me. The woman held the door open, and as I passed her, I looked into her face. It had bright pink lipstick, and its mouth was still turned down. I couldn't tell whether it meant anger, or sadness, or something else. Then I looked down from her face and saw her bosom, which was very large and also too big for her dress. I felt alarmed, and my head turned itself to the side.

The room she led us into was small and gray and brown, with lots of squares and rectangles in it—filing cabinets and desks and piles of papers. It did not look very clean. I worried about germs. The woman leaned against the square of one of the desks.

"So," she said to Salim. "I'm Sarah. I'm the manager here. But you know that, right? I'm sure Gloria told you. She's sent you to make sure things are OK after the police visited, right?" The corners of her mouth went up. "You know," she added, "you've got the same kind of funny accent as Gloria. You British?"

"Manchester," said Salim. "Ted and Kat are from London. But—you're sure you talked to Mum?"

"If your mom's Gloria McCloud, then yes. She called on Monday to book a van for yesterday morning at ten-forty to pick an item up from the Guggenheim back entrance on Eighty-Ninth Street. She said that it would be all boxed up in the loading bay, ready to go. We don't ask questions at Effortless, so I said fine."

I felt very strange. Sarah was sure that the person she had spoken to on the phone had been Aunt Gloria. She was also sure that Aunt Gloria really had stolen a painting—and that we were helping her. This was not right. I wanted to say something. Then Kat kicked me. When I looked over at her, she was shaking her head. I understood that she was telling me not to say anything.

"She gave me her credit-card details and that was it," said Sarah. "I guess you want that receipt, hmm? I've got it here. I told the police I couldn't find it." She opened a drawer of one of the filing cabinets and flicked through it. It didn't look in order, which was bad business practice. "Here you go," she said after a few minutes. "Look. Dated the sixth of this month, at three-fifteen p.m."

I thought. Today was the tenth, Friday. The sixth had been Monday.

Salim's mouth was turned far down, and I saw that his hand was shaking as he took the receipt and put it in his pocket. Then he quickly raised his camera and took a photograph of Sarah, with the office behind her.

"Hey!" said Sarah, holding up her hand, which had pink-painted nails. "No photos of me, all right? Look, I don't know why your mom's sent you here so soon— but you tell her that everything went as she planned it.

I mean, my driver got there a few minutes early, but the crate was already there. So he picked it up and drove back here, and we passed it straight on to the next driver."

"The *next*?" asked Kat.

"That's what Gloria asked for," said Sarah. "A guy from Elephant Moving in Queens came to get it. He had his instructions too—also from your mom. Everything was in order. So we handed it over. That's the last we saw of it. I told the police it had been picked up, but said I couldn't remember the details and couldn't find the paperwork. Hope that threw them off the scent for a while. You can tell your mom that we sure held up our end of the deal."

I was very upset. Sarah was saying that she had lied to the police, and she thought that the person who had hired her to lie was Aunt Gloria. I did not want to believe it. I did not want to be in her office anymore. I wanted to get away from it as fast as I could.

I also wanted Mum there, to tell us what to do. But Mum was not there. We were on our own, in Brooklyn, and our first clue had led to some upsetting answers. Aunt Gloria's credit card had paid for the pickup. A woman with a British accent had ordered the van. The person who had taken the call, Sarah, thought that Aunt

Gloria was guilty. And she had told us that the crate, with *In the Black Square* in it, had been sent on to Queens, which I knew was almost the opposite side of New York to Brooklyn. We were in the wrong place after all. When I looked at Salim's down-turned face, I knew that he felt very upset as well.

"You OK, kids?" asked Sarah. "Do you need anything else? Otherwise, I've got a lot to do. You can show yourselves out, right?"

23

SUBWAY BLUES

We walked back to the subway without saying anything. I matched my walk to Salim's again, so that we could keep on being Ted-and-Salim. Salim turned his head and smiled at me, but I was worried that he was making his face lie again. I couldn't see what he had to be happy about.

Hurricane Kat hit when we were halfway between East Broadway and Delancey Street.

"THIS CAN'T BE IT!" she shouted, waving her arms.

"Quiet, kid!" said the old man sitting on the silver metal seat opposite us. Kat made a rude face.

"No," she repeated. "This can't be it, Salim! I don't

believe it! Auntie Glo wouldn't steal a painting. We *know* her! I know that Sarah *thinks* she did it, but that's not like Auntie Glo! Whoever *really* did it is framing her."

"But Sarah said the person who called had a British accent," said Salim. He was sitting hunched forward with his hands dangling between his knees. I hunched forward as well, to keep on copying him.

"Exactly! Anyone could *pretend* to be British," said Kat. "Look—it's not hard for someone to frame Auntie Glo. Anyone at the Guggenheim who knows her knows her accent. And they also know how scatty she is. She's always leaving things around, isn't she? Someone could easily have taken her card out of her handbag while she wasn't paying attention on Monday and used it to call the moving companies from her work telephone, and also to buy the smoke bombs. And we know more than we did before. We know that the call was made on Monday afternoon, and we know that the caller gave an exact time for the pickup yesterday. So they already knew when the robbery would happen—this was planned for when they knew the museum would be almost empty, and when Auntie Glo would be in it. She told everyone we were coming, didn't she? And when she was going to show us around. Lionel *said* we were expected, didn't he?

So I bet the *real* thief heard and decided it would be the perfect opportunity to steal the painting and frame her."

"Frame her," I repeated. *Frame* is a good word that, according to my dictionary, means producing false evidence against a person to pretend they are guilty. Pictures can also be framed, literally not metaphorically. I thought about *In the Black Square,* and the way it looked as though it had not one frame but two. Kat was making sense, and I thought that her hypotheses were good.

"Exactly, Ted," said Kat. "Exactly! And that means we really need to help Aunt Gloria. Someone *planned* this! We can't just give up! Come *on*! Think!"

I thought.

"What if Sarah was the person who stole the painting?"

I thought this was a good idea, but Salim sat up and shook his head. "No, Ted," he said. "It must have been someone in the museum, like we've already said, because of the telephone and the credit card, and the fact that they must have known her password. We'd have noticed Sarah if she was there yesterday too, and I think she *thought* she was telling the truth about Mum. No, I think she's just a bit shady—sorry, Ted, I mean she's not very honest. She was happy to help the thief steal a painting, wasn't she?"

I thought that Effortless Light Moving, with its dark staircase and dim office, *was* a shady place to be.

"And if the real thief knew about Effortless Light Moving, that means they knew how to steal things. They really knew what they were doing!" said Kat. "Auntie Glo wouldn't have any idea. Look—we can narrow our suspect list down because now we know *when* the thief used Auntie Glo's credit card, and we know that Effortless Light received the call from a phone number at the Guggenheim. The person who took the card, and the painting, has to have been at the Guggenheim yesterday *and* on Monday—or at least they must have made the telephone call then, and gone through her bag to get the card details before that."

"YES!" shouted Salim. He slapped his palm against Kat's, and then Kat punched me on the arm. It hurt.

"OW!" I said.

The train rattled. Underground lights flashed past the window. "Shush!" said a young woman with glasses.

"Listen," said Kat, more quietly. Her eyes were wide. "There's no point chasing after the painting. If it can be found, the police will find it. So we've got to focus on working out *who* really stole it, not *where* it is."

Kat was right. We knew two very important things

about the thief: that they were one of the people working in the Guggenheim on the day the painting was stolen, and that they had been near enough to Aunt Gloria to take her credit card from her purse and then call the moving company on Monday afternoon. That had been after the conversation I had overheard between Mum and Dad about us going to New York, and after Aunt Gloria had planned our trip, including our visit to the Guggenheim, so the real thief had known then that Aunt Gloria would be in the Guggenheim on Thursday morning. Therefore, we were looking for someone who had been at the Guggenheim on Thursday, and also who'd had access to Aunt Gloria's bag to steal her card on Monday.

Salim rubbed his hands across his face and blinked.

"You really think we can do this?" he asked quietly.

"We've got Ted," said Kat. "He's our secret weapon. I bet the police don't have anyone like him."

I watched Salim's mouth. After four seconds its corners finally turned upward. "We do have Ted," he said.

"And we've got *you*," said Kat. "You know the Guggenheim, right? You know the people who work there, and where to find them today. You know who our suspects are!"

She got her notebook out of her leopard-skin backpack

and turned to the list we had made a few hours ago. I saw that we could make a new list to show who we thought were suspects, and who we had ruled out. We took Aunt Gloria, Sandra and the fire crew off, and that left us with eight people. Kat wrote them all out, in pen, in her notebook.

This is what we now had:

WHO COULD HAVE STOLEN THE PAINTING?

1. Lionel (security guard). The second-to-last person to leave the museum. Because he is the security guard, he must know how to shut down the burglar alarms and security cameras, and we know they were down yesterday morning.
2. Helen (head of the maintenance crew). Third last to leave.
3. Jacob (member of the maintenance crew). Fourth last.
4. Ty (member of the maintenance crew). Fifth last.
5. Lana (member of the maintenance crew). Third person out of the museum after us. Less likely to be her, though we can't rule her out yet.
6. Ben (member of the maintenance crew). Came first out of the museum after us. He was also

with Rafael. Does this rule him out? Less likely to be him, though we can't rule him out yet.

7. Rafael (janitor). Came first out of the museum after us. He was also with Ben. Does this rule him out? Less likely to be him, though we can't rule him out yet either.

8. Gabriel (builder). This is very unlikely. He was working on the outside of the building and never went inside. Although he might have climbed in through the broken skylight to steal the painting. This is Ted's idea. We need to test it to see if it is possible. Gabriel was also late for the roll call, which is suspicious.

WHO HAS BEEN RULED OUT?

Aunt Gloria (because she is being framed), Sandra (because she is too small to have carried the painting, and also she was wearing very high heels), the fire crew (because none of them could have been at the Guggenheim on Monday).

"Good," said Kat. "Right. We've got to interview our suspects and work out which one is guilty. We need you, Salim."

I was glad that Kat seemed to have stopped being Mean Kat, now that we were working on this case. She had told Salim a kind thing that he needed to hear.

The train pulled into Delancey Street. Seven people got out of our carriage, and nine got on. "Come on, Salim," said Kat. "Where do we go first?"

Salim's face firmed up. He lifted his shoulders. "We're going to see Ty," he said.

24
BUILDING A CASE

We got off the F train at Broadway–Lafayette Street, which was back in Manhattan. Everywhere we went, New York seemed like a different city. I imagined us like Odysseus, traveling to different islands and facing a different task on each one. I wondered what we would find here.

This street was very wide, and striped with white lines that told people where to cross. There were large flat billboards sticking up into the sky, covered in pictures of people with no expressions on their faces. Traffic lights hung in the air as well, on curved yellow-and-white poles. The buildings behind the boards and the lights were big and brown, with lots of windows. I counted only three trees, which was a bad thing. There are not enough trees in New York. Trees are good, because during the process of photosynthesis, in the daytime, they take in carbon dioxide (which is what human beings breathe out every four seconds on average) and give out oxygen. I imagined New York like a seesaw (this is a simile), with all the people on one side, and the trees on the other. It did not balance out. As a future meteorologist, I was concerned by this.

I noticed that the air smelled rotten and there were dirty stains on the edges of the road. "Kat!" I said. "This place is not very hygienic."

"Save it, Ted," said Kat. "Follow Salim—come on!"

Salim was moving very fast. He has long legs, and this means that he can walk more quickly than I can. Kat is almost as tall as he is, but she was trying to wait for me. Then she got tired of waiting and grabbed my arm, dragging me forward.

"Hrumm!" I said urgently.

"Save it, Ted!" snapped Kat again. "We don't have time!"

I looked at my weather watch. It was 1:17 p.m. New York time, which meant that it was 6:17 p.m. in London. I thought that we did have time, plenty of it. I imagined the two times next to each other, as though we could balance between them, in two places at once, and it felt good. But I couldn't explain this to Kat, and so I had to hurry after her, my school-uniform shirt itching my arms, all the way to a very tall white building with glass windows and sliding glass doors. Salim was waiting for us, his face wrinkled up and cheeks red.

"This is the Center for Architecture," he panted. "Ty messaged me this morning—he's working here today while the police have the Guggenheim shut down."

We went through the glass doors into a rush of coolness that flowed down from the top of my head to my fingertips. It felt good. But there were several people looking at us, which was less good.

"Hurry!" muttered Salim.

One of the women, in a purple dress and a hairstyle that looked not real—like a cumulus cloud formation glued to her head—came up to us.

"What are you doing here, young man?" she asked Salim.

I opened my mouth to tell her, but Kat spoke first. "We're here to see our father," she said in a loud voice.

"And what is your father's name?" asked the woman.

I saw Kat's eyes flicker and then settle on something

behind the woman's head. It was a glass board covered in names. I began to read them, *A* to *Z*. I was only on *C* when Kat said, "Norman Ruby."

"Oh!" said the woman, her eyes wide. "I didn't know—"

"He doesn't talk about us much," said Kat, lowering her voice. "We're from his *first* marriage."

"Oh!" said the woman, and her cheeks turned red.

"Yes," I said. "And Salim is our friend, not our cousin."

This was the fifth lie I have ever told.

The woman looked at me strangely, but she said to Salim, "Well, if you're with them—go on, then. Young lady, your father's in his office."

"Thank you," said Kat politely. Her face was very calm. "Come on, Ted and Salim." We walked up a ramp, and through some sliding glass doors, and then Kat's face slipped into a grin that made her whole face wobble. "Ted!" she squawked, leaning against a wall and putting her hands on her stomach. "You nearly gave us away! *Salim is our friend, not our cousin!*"

Salim laughed too, leaning against Kat.

"Where is Ty?" I asked. "Is he studying to be an architect here?"

"Not exactly," said Salim. "I mean—yeah, one day.

That's the plan. He's saving up. But right now he's just their electrician."

We found Ty at the end of a long marble corridor. He was wearing dark red coveralls and a baseball cap over his big hairstyle, and he was working on a panel of wires that stuck out of the wall. He looked up and saw us, and a smile appeared on his face.

"Salim!" he said. "Kat and Ted! Hey! What're you doing here?"

I wondered whether Salim would lie this time, but he didn't. "We're here about the painting," he said. "Ty—Mum's been arrested."

Ty's face stopped smiling. His lips pursed up small, and his eyes narrowed. "Are you sure?" he asked.

"We were there!" said Salim. "She's been taken away by that detective. But, Ty, she didn't do it! She's being framed. We know she is. We're trying to work out who did it."

"Salim," said Ty quietly. "Man. Don't get involved with the police, OK? This is their business. They'll most likely drop it once they can't get any leads. Your mom's respectable. They won't be able to hold her."

"Yeah, but we can't take that chance!" said Salim, his eyes very wide. "And the detective who took her away—I could tell he didn't trust her. You've got to help us! We know that the person who framed her was at the Guggenheim on Monday. Do you know who was working there that day?"

"Sorry, man, I can't help you there," said Ty, wrinkling up his forehead as he thought hard. "Monday I was here from eight until six, working with another member of the crew. Then I went home. Didn't go near the museum."

Salim looked pleased. Kat got out her notebook and wrote in it.

"As for yesterday—well, I was there, but I didn't see nothing. I was on the ramp on the second level. The lights had gone out there, so I was fixing them. When the alarm went off, I—man, I froze. Salim, you know I'm no tough guy. My legs went stiff. I was stuck halfway up my ladder, and there was smoke everywhere. I don't know how long I was there. Then I heard Helen yelling for us all to get out, and I could move again. I got down off that ladder and ran down the ramp."

"You didn't run into anyone else on the ramp?" asked Salim.

Ty's frown got bigger. "I stuck close to the edge so I

could feel my way down," he said. "Sandra was standing at the main door, bugging us the way she always does. And I heard Jacob shouting behind me. I don't know where anyone else was, though. I lost them. I know that your mom was the last one out—I remember that."

I thought about this story. It fitted with what I had seen in the Guggenheim, and with when Ty had come out of the museum entrance.

"And you didn't see anyone set off the smoke bombs?" asked Kat, her eyebrows pulling together. "Maybe carrying a strange parcel or bag that the smoke bombs might have been kept in?"

Ty shook his head. "No way," he said. "I was focused on what I was doing. I couldn't figure out what had made the lights go out—still can't. We're all due to go back in tomorrow, if the police have cleared out by then.

"Look, there's not much more I can say. If you're sure that it wasn't your mom—well, I get it. But you know who I bet can help? Jacob. He was way up above, working on the fourth level of the ramp—he could look down on the rest of us. I bet he saw something!"

"Where is he?" asked Kat.

"Well," said Ty, and he smiled, for the first time since he had started to talk. "We all have second jobs, right?

I fix electrics anywhere that'll have me. Jacob plays in a band."

"No way!" said Salim. "He never told me that!"

"Oh, just you wait and see," said Ty. He bent over his work, beaming at a joke I could not understand.

25

ZUM SCHNEIDER

The pressure in the air was very high. The sun reflected off the pavement and shot into my eyes as Kat zipped open her backpack, put on her sunglasses and tipped her head back to drink from her water bottle. A drop of water escaped and trickled down her cheek as she tilted her head, and she wiped it away. Even in New York, gravity still pulled water droplets, and human beings, down.

Suddenly I heard music. We followed the sound until we were standing outside a building with a blue-and-white-checked flag hanging from its left-hand side.

"This is it!" said Salim. "ZUM SCHNEIDER. GERMAN RESTAURANT AND BAVARIAN OOMPAH MUSIC VENUE. How weird!"

The front door swished open as a man stepped outside and the music blared out with him, along with a thumping like a heartbeat that made my feet wobble on the pavement. The sun was in my eyes, and my ears were full of noise.

"Hrumm," I said.

"Ted," said Kat. "*Ted!* I know you don't like it, but it'll be all right. Come on. We just have to go inside for one minute."

"Actually one minute?" I asked.

"*Actually* one minute," said Kat. "Count, if you like."

So I counted.

One. Two. Three. Salim opened the door, and Kat pushed me forward, and we were in a hot noisy space that smelled like Dad's beer bottles. "Hrumm," I said urgently, and my hand shook itself out. *Six. Seven. Eight.*

There were people sitting at tables, shouting and clapping and stamping their feet on the floor. *Eighteen. Nineteen. Twenty.*

There were five people right in front of us. They were all dressed in blue overalls with embroidered flowers on them, and they were playing shiny gold musical instruments. The loud, brassy music was coming from them. I imagined that I could see the notes floating out of their wide gold mouths. I kept counting. *Thirty-five. Thirty-six. Thirty-seven.*

I looked at the musicians and I realized that I knew one of them. The old, white-bearded man with his arms wrapped around a huge golden tuba had been in the Guggenheim the day before. He had been wearing different clothes then, and his face had had a different expression too, but I could still smell the paint coming off him through the beer smell and the music. This was Jacob.

Salim waved his hands and shouted, going up to the man. I counted. *Forty-seven. Forty-eight. Forty-nine.*

The man put down the tuba. His mouth opened in surprise, and he turned and said something to the man next to him. *Fifty-six. Fifty-seven.*

Then he was standing up and walking toward us, flapping his hands, and then the four of us were back outside, and the door closed behind us, and the German music was muffled.

Sixty. I breathed out.

The man put his hands on his hips. He was not smiling.

"What the heck are you doing here?" he asked.

26

OOMPAH AND ORCHESTRA

Jacob was angry. I could tell this because, under the wrinkles of his face, his eyes were narrowed and his mouth was small too.

"How did you find me, Salim?" he asked. His voice was deep and scratchy. "No, wait, I know—you've been talking to Ty. When I get my hands on him, I swear— Come on, you can't be here, and you can't bring other kids here either. We aren't on museum time now, so I've got nothing to do with you. And don't tease me about what I do."

"You're a musician in a German folk band!" said Salim. His cheeks were twitching and his eyes glittered. "I didn't know!"

"It isn't funny," said Jacob. "I knew you'd make it a joke. You and Ty, always teasing me. You shouldn't hang around with him. I do what I can for money, all right? I've got a grandson in second grade and a granddaughter in fifth. That girl! Last month she tells me she wants to be a concert pianist."

"Hey, I didn't mean to joke," said Salim. "I think it's cool that you're musical, all right? I just never imagined you as part of a band, especially one like *this*."

"You should see my tips," said Jacob, and his cheeks wrinkled suddenly. "That's what I've been telling my granddaughter. Who wants to play in an orchestra when you could be in an oompah band? Now, who's this, then? Your girlfriend?"

I was surprised that Jacob didn't recognize me and Kat. He had been standing next to us at the Guggenheim the day before. But now he was squinting at us, and I wondered if he could not see us properly.

"EW!" said Kat, so loudly that it made my ears hum. "I'm his cousin, thank you very much, and so's Ted!"

"So, whatcha want?" asked Jacob. "I've got five minutes' grace before our next number. Spill."

"It's the painting," said Salim. *"In the Black Square."*

"Yeah, it got stolen," said Jacob. "Nothing to do with

me." His body had tightened up and his feet stepped back from us.

"Yeah, but someone stole Mum's credit-card number and used it to hire the van that helped steal it," said Salim. "The police have arrested her because they think she did it, but I *know* she didn't. So it must have been someone else at the museum."

"Were you at the Guggenheim on Monday afternoon?" asked Kat, very quickly. Her eyebrows were lowered again and her eyes were narrowed.

"Me?" said Jacob. His mouth went down even more, and his wrinkles deepened until they made shadows in his face. Body language is how detectives can tell who is behaving suspiciously. I hoped that Kat and Salim were watching for it. "No. And don't you give me that look, missy. My granddaughter had a concert at school on Monday, and she made me come along and accompany her. I was stuck with a hundred kids and their parents from one until almost five. Look!"

He reached into his pocket and pulled out a crumpled flyer, which he held out to us. It read GREENVIEW ELEMENTARY SCHOOL MUSIC CONCERT. The date at the top was Monday, August 6.

"I didn't have anything to do with yesterday either. I

was up on the fourth level, with everyone else below me. I just remember looking down and seeing that smoke coming up at me. It was so fast, like a monster. Like something from a movie. I thought I was gonna die. Living around here, you're always ready for something like that, but having it happen—it was different. I put my hand on the side of the ramp and walked down through the smoke. The feeling when I came out into the sun!"

He spread his hands out, palms up. I liked the idea that the smoke had been a monster. It made what had happened sound more like a story, or a part of *The Odyssey*.

"So, no, I didn't see anything," Jacob said. "And I don't want anything to do with this. I can't help your mom, or you. Why don't you go pester Helen Wu? She's at the Museum of Modern Art today. She works repair in lots of different places, and today she's there."

And with that, he stuffed the crumpled flyer back in his pocket, turned and went back inside.

27

FIGURE OF SPEECH IN A BUN

"So Jacob is ruled out as well," said Kat to Salim. She was scribbling in her notebook again. "Unless his alibi is a lie! Though that flyer looked real. Ted, what do you think?"

"Hrumm," I said thoughtfully. "He needs money."

"Exactly," said Kat. "For his granddaughter!"

I shook my head.

"What, Ted?" asked Kat.

"Jacob's voice," I said. "It's too deep. He couldn't make himself sound like a woman. And, Kat, he didn't recognize us, even though he saw us yesterday. I think that he can't see very well."

"Ted, that's good!" said Salim. "Well done! It's true—Ty's told me that Helen's been getting mad at Jacob because his work's slipping. If he can't see properly, that would explain it. But if he can't see properly—"

"There's no way he could have carried the painting through the museum in the smoke!" said Kat. "He's small too, and old. It would be too difficult for him. I think we just ruled him out! Amazing!"

Kat began to smile, and so did Salim. At that moment we were Kat-and-Salim-and-Ted, a real team. It felt good.

WHO COULD HAVE STOLEN THE PAINTING?

1. Lionel (security guard). The second-to-last person to leave the museum. Because he is the security guard, he must know how to shut down the burglar alarms and security cameras, and we know they were down yesterday morning.
2. Helen (head of the maintenance crew). Third last to leave.
3. ~~Jacob (member of the maintenance crew). Fourth last.~~
4. ~~Ty (member of the maintenance crew). Fifth last.~~
5. Lana (member of the maintenance crew). Third

person out of the museum after us. Less likely to be her, though we can't rule her out yet.

6. Ben (member of the maintenance crew). Came first out of the museum after us. He was also with Rafael. Does this rule him out? Less likely to be him, though we can't rule him out yet.

7. Rafael (janitor). Came first out of the museum after us. He was also with Ben. Does this rule him out? Less likely to be him, though we can't rule him out yet either.

8. Gabriel (builder). This is very unlikely. He was working on the outside of the building and never went inside. Although he might have climbed in through the broken skylight to steal the painting. This is Ted's idea. We need to test it to see if it is possible. Gabriel was also late for the roll call, which is suspicious.

WHO HAS BEEN RULED OUT?

Aunt Gloria (because she is being framed), Sandra (because she is too small to have carried the painting, and also she was wearing very high heels), the fire crew (because none of them could have been

at the Guggenheim on Monday), Ty (because he was
not near the museum on Monday afternoon), Jacob
(because he could not pretend to be a woman on
the telephone; also, his eyesight is too bad for him
to have been able to carry the painting through the
museum and he has an alibi for Monday afternoon).

We went back to the subway, and came out in another new part of New York. This one was louder and more full of people than I had seen so far.

"It's like a river!" said Kat, pushing the sweaty hair off her forehead. I thought it just looked like a very wide road, with cars and yellow taxis jammed up against each other, honking their horns. People were also rushing down the pavement toward us. They were all in black and gray, with sunglasses on, and they all seemed as though they would run straight into me. I put my hands up over my ears and groaned to keep out the noise. I remembered Odysseus putting wax in his ears so he could not hear the Sirens singing. I took twenty long deep breaths, and then I could move again.

Salim and Kat stopped at a hot dog cart on the side of the road. The air around it smelled very strong, and very old. The cart was striped red and yellow, and it was surrounded by five orange traffic cones to stop the traffic coming too close to it. I looked at the cones, and then Salim put a hot dog into my left hand.

Salim had just ketchup on his hot dog. Mine had nothing on it at all. Kat had mustard and ketchup on hers, but she ate around the bun, in little bites, as though her mouth was too small for it. She squashed the rest of the bun into her palm and threw it into a dustbin.

"Aren't you hungry, Kat?" I asked.

"No!" said Kat, jutting her chin. "Aren't *you* hungry?"

I was still holding my hot dog. I had only taken two bites of it.

"Ted, you know hot dogs aren't really dogs, right?" asked Salim.

"I know," I said. "*Hot dog* is a figure of speech for a food that is ground-up meat parts in a bun. I am just not very hungry."

"Ugh, TED!" shrieked Kat.

Salim laughed. "I've missed you, Ted," he said. "You're brilliant."

What Salim meant was not that I was shiny, but that I was good. And that made me glad, because I was sure now that Salim and I *were* still friends.

28

GLASS GARDEN

The Museum of Modern Art, where Helen Wu, the woman with the ponytail from the Guggenheim maintenance crew, was working, is on West Fifty-Third Street. From the outside it does not look special, like the Guggenheim. It is just a gray glass box shape pushed into a shiny black building, at the bottom of a shiny black skyscraper. I saw the three of us in the black glass as we walked by, Kat glittering and bony, with her hair scraped up on her head, Salim with his green shirt and set face and me in my gray uniform. I am always surprised when I see myself in a mirror. What is inside my head never fits with what is on the outside of me. I look small in mirrors, and I looked very small here, almost lost among the other tourists, and short next to Kat and Salim. I stared at myself until Kat shouted at me to move.

We went through a big square hall and up some stairs. There in front of us was a garden inside glass. It did not look as though it belonged there. I imagined someone cutting out a square of museum with a huge sharp knife and gluing in a square of garden. It was a strange thought, and it made me feel as though I was trying to look at two things at once. Salim led us into the garden, and in the middle was a fountain. In front of it was a paving stone with a large crack, surrounded by orange cones, which I knew were code for *Be careful*. This stone was being fixed, and Helen was fixing it.

Helen Wu's hair was in the same thick black ponytail as yesterday and she was wearing overalls. Her tools were piled next to her—boxes of nails and screws and other things I did not know the names for. Her eyes as she turned to look at us were narrowed. There was a redhaired woman beside her, who was shorter and rounder, wearing the same kind of overalls. I thought she looked familiar, and then I realized that this was someone else I knew from the Guggenheim crew: Lana, who had been with Helen yesterday. She looked at us, then at Helen, and stepped backward.

"Salim," Helen said. "What are you doing here?"

"We've come about Mum," said Salim. I saw Salim's hands shaking and I had a theory that he was nervous. Perhaps I had this theory because I also felt nervous.

Helen Wu was standing very upright, with her mouth in a thin line and her arms folded. Her body was saying *Be careful*, just like the cones. "She stole that painting," she said.

"No!" said Salim. "It isn't true."

"She paid for the moving van that took it away," said Helen Wu, raising one black eyebrow.

"Her card paid for it," admitted Salim. "But she didn't do it. She's being framed."

"Why does everyone know that? About the van?" Kat asked Helen, sticking out her chin. "Did Sandra tell you?"

"Sandra?" said Helen. "Why would *she* bother to tell us anything? She might act nice to *you*, but when Gloria's not around, she's a total—"

"Helen, *don't!*" said Lana behind her, and Helen shut her mouth.

So Lana and Helen were a team, I thought. They worked together, just the way Salim and Kat and I did.

And Helen did not appear to like Aunt Gloria or Sandra. That was also a useful thing to have learned.

"Anyway," Helen went on, "everyone's talking about it. Someone from the police told one of the Eighteenth Street firefighters that Gloria was about to be arrested, and Ben heard about it from them and told us."

I wondered how this could be—but Helen was still talking.

"Satisfied?" she asked. "And yes, I think Gloria did it. She was the last person out of the museum. When the smoke started, I saw her up by the gallery where *In the Black Square* was. Seems clear to me."

She was right about where Aunt Gloria had been standing. She had been there with us when the alarm had gone off. But we knew that, all the same, Aunt Gloria had not done it.

"We were working on the ramp," said Helen. "I was cutting a false wall down to size, and Lana was helping."

"False wall?" asked Kat. Kat had forgotten what Aunt Gloria had told Mum on Thursday, but I had not.

"We do it for most of the exhibitions, to make sure the space fits the paintings," said Helen. "Your aunt asked for it for a few of the bigger ones. Your aunt asks for a lot of things. And before you ask, Lana and I were together the whole time yesterday, right until we came out the door. Weren't we, Lana?"

"Yes, Helen," said Lana. But her arms were wrapped round her stomach, and she was slightly hunched over. Her body and her mouth were not saying the same thing. Was she lying? Was I getting better at knowing when people are not telling the truth?

I thought back to yesterday morning. I remembered the smoke. Lana had come out, then Sandra, then Ty, Jacob and finally Helen. Helen *was* lying, and so was Lana. They had not come out together after all.

"Oh!" I said loudly. I wanted to tell Salim and Kat what I had discovered. But Salim was shaking his head at me. He did not want me to speak yet.

Kat was staring very hard at Helen Wu. I stared at her too. I saw that a few strands of wiry black hair had come out of Helen's ponytail, above her left ear. I saw that the collar of her shirt was neatly pressed. But although I had been able to see Lana's lie, I could not see whatever it was Kat saw.

"Did you fix anything at the Guggenheim earlier this week?" Kat asked. "On Monday, maybe?"

Helen paused for a moment. "Yes, I did. There was a broken drinking fountain on the first floor that day. . . ." She glared at Lana. "Gloria was complaining about it, so Sandra called me to fix it, even though it was my day off.

It was a one-person job, and I was done by four. Frankly, I hardly needed to be there. Lana wasn't with me."

"I was . . . busy," said Lana, and she looked away. "All day."

This was very interesting. Helen had been in the museum on Monday. She could have taken Aunt Gloria's credit card, used it to call Effortless Light Moving and then put it back in Aunt Gloria's bag. She was a woman, so her voice would sound right.

But although Lana had said she was not at the museum, I was not convinced. She hadn't explained where she really was, and I thought that was strange.

"All right," said Salim. "Thanks, Helen. Thanks, Lana. Come on, Kat, Ted." He took Kat by the elbow and led her out of the garden, back into the museum. Salim leaned against the inside of the glass box as tourists rushed by. "What about that?" he asked.

"Helen was definitely in the Guggenheim on Monday!" said Kat. "She could easily have stolen Auntie Glo's credit card, and made the call too. Lana was obviously lying for her about yesterday."

"Yes, she was," I agreed. "They did not come out together. Helen came out much later than Lana did."

"Nice memory, Ted!" said Salim. He held up his hand. I thought carefully, and then I held up my hand as well, and Salim slapped his palm against mine. I was proud of myself.

"What if—OK, what if Helen stole the painting?" Kat asked. She opened her notebook and looked at the pages of it. "After all, Helen's story doesn't make sense. She was below Ty on the ramp, but he came out before her. Isn't that strange? Why wouldn't he see her?"

Kat was right.

"Salim, text Ty!" said Kat. "Ask him whether she was there!"

Salim got out his phone and turned it on again. It buzzed seven times, and Salim made a face. "Sandra's been leaving loads of messages," he said. "Er, I think we're going to be in trouble."

"Don't worry about that!" said Kat. "Just text Ty!"

Salim did, his fingers making patterns across the phone keys. I thought about the way that he knew which buttons to press to make the words he wanted. It was another translation, just like English into American or symbols into weather. We waited, then the phone buzzed again.

Salim showed us the text message:

Didnt see H but cant be sure. So smoky. Why?

"So she wasn't on the ramp!" he said excitedly. "That means she might have been in the tower gallery, stealing the painting!"

Salim was making a *leap of logic*. This is when something is *probably* true, at least 51 percent, so someone assumes that it is 100 percent true.

I said, "Hrumm!" and Kat laughed and said, "Ted isn't sure. Right, Ted? But it's a good lead. And what about Lana? What she said about Monday was weird too, wasn't it? Why wouldn't she tell us where she really was?"

"It was weird," I agreed. "What if she did not want to tell us because she *was* at the Guggenheim?"

Kat and Salim nodded.

"But she was one of the first people to come out yesterday," said Kat, looking at her list. "We don't think she would have had enough time to steal the painting."

This was a good point.

"Wait!" said Salim. "What if—what if Lana and Helen were working together? What if they *helped each other* steal the painting?"

"Salim!" said Kat. "That's—it could be! I could see they were good friends, just now."

I remembered what I had thought earlier, about Helen and Lana being a team. I was pleased that Kat and I had come to the same conclusion.

She scribbled excitedly in her notebook. "What if Lana snuck in and stole Auntie Glo's card while Helen distracted her? And then Helen stole the painting yesterday, and Lana lied to cover it up?"

This was more than a leap of logic. Kat was telling a story.

"I don't think we can know that yet, Kat," I said.

"I know, Ted," sighed Kat. "But we can't rule it out! We think that *one* person stole the painting, don't we? It'd be risky to tell anyone you were going to steal a painting—unless you were good friends, just like Helen and Lana."

Salim's phone buzzed. "It's Ty again. He says *Good luck,*" said Salim, his lips curving up. "All right, Kat, I'll turn off the phone."

"Where do we go next?" I asked.

"Union Square," said Salim. "We've got to talk to Ben."

29

SWEET FOURTEEN

As we sat on the subway, the woman behind us began to talk to her friend.

"Yeah!" she said. "I know! Marty's so dumb. I said eighteenth. *Eighteenth!* Come on, who'd want a Harry Potter cake for their *eightieth* birthday?"

"Aw," said her friend. "I'm sorry."

Salim's eyes went wide, and his hands dropped down onto his camera. The train jolted as it came into the Twenty-Third Street station, and the doors clanked open, creating a convection current that sent a rush of cool air out and a rush of hot air in. "Quick!" he said. "Get up! Get off the train!"

"Why?" Kat gasped. But even though her voice wasn't certain, her body was already moving. She jumped up, her feather earrings dancing and her leopard-skin backpack swinging like a deadly weapon. I had to duck to stop it hitting my head.

"Hey!" I said. I looked down and saw the dirty linoleum of the train, then a silver gap between the train and the platform, and then the tiles of the platform itself as we leaped out. The train doors closed like pincers biting together.

"What's wrong?" Kat asked Salim.

"Nothing!" said Salim. "I just had an idea when that woman said *eighteenth*. Remember the fire engine from yesterday? It had to come from downtown, because all the closer fire engines were busy, which is why it took a few minutes for them to get to the museum. And remember what Helen said about the fire crew? She said they were from Eighteenth Street—that's what I just remembered. Well, we should go there now!"

"Good idea, Salim!" said Kat.

My heartbeat was fast, but I was not just nervous. I was excited too. This case was not what I had expected. It was an adventure like Odysseus's, and I realized that I was enjoying it.

The Eighteenth Street fire station was on a narrow street with very high buildings on each side of the road. In New York, fire stations are not in buildings on their own. They are just built into the bottoms of skyscrapers, because there is no extra room. This fire station was set into the wall, with a concrete ramp down to the dirty road. At the top of the ramp was a big red-and-silver engine. It didn't look like a fire engine in London does. Its license plate said SWEET 14 and there was a large red-and-white 14 on its grille. I could see us reflected in the two large clear windows at the front of the fire engine.

A white man in a blue shirt and gray-and-yellow trousers was wiping down its side. He was moving his arm slowly and carefully, in big arcs. He had big muscles, a shaved head and lots of freckles on his face and arms. He looked up and saw us, and Salim, who was holding up his camera to take a picture. "Hey!" he said, his eyes crinkling. "What are you kids doing? You lost?"

"Actually," said Kat, flicking her hair, "we're here to talk to you. We've got some questions."

"Say that again," said the man in his deep voice.

Kat did. I was worried. I thought the man was about to tell us to go away.

But I was wrong. "Hey!" he said again. His eyes widened. "Are you from *England*?"

"We all are," I told him. "My sister, Kat, and I are from London, and Salim is from Manchester, although—"

"You're from *London*? Hey! I used to live there! I mean, in another life, before you kids were even thought about. But that's great! I'm Hank Katz, by the way."

I considered the words *in another life*. I decided that they must be a figure of speech. Hank Katz did not look like a person who had been reincarnated or brought back from the dead. I also considered the name Hank Katz. It seemed familiar to me, just like this man. But I could not remember why.

"Hi!" said Kat.

"You guys just have the *best* accent. I always loved the English accent," said Hank. Now he was smiling. We had made him happy. This was good from the point of view of our investigation. "So, what's up?"

"We're tourists," said Kat, putting her hand on Salim's arm. This seemed to be a signal. Salim looked down at the hand, and then up again at Kat's face, and did not say anything. "We were up by the Guggenheim yesterday, and I think we saw your fire engine! I mean, we were just wandering past today and we recognized its number, so we thought we'd say hi!"

"Yeah?"

"Yes!" Kat said.

"What Kat means is that we've come about—" I began. This time Salim kicked me. I realized then that we were lying, and stopped speaking.

"You were up at the Guggenheim?" asked Hank. He frowned. "Wait. You're not something to do with the police, are you?"

"We're *kids,*" said Kat, her eyes very wide. "What do you mean, the police?"

Kat was acting. This was very clever of her. I was glad that Hank hadn't had a good look at us yesterday, the way the maintenance crew members had. He did not recognize us, or know that we were lying.

"A painting got stolen yesterday," explained Hank. "The person who did it's been arrested now, so I guess it doesn't really matter. But it was the weirdest thing. We got called because of a fire, but when we went in, there wasn't one. Just two canisters of smoke, one in the stairwell and one at the bottom of the ramp. I've seen that kind before—I've used them when I go paintballing. Harmless. Don't mark anything—just cover everything for ten minutes. We ran around checking the building, and then we came out again. I even stuck my head in the tower gallery, but I never noticed the painting was gone. Feel bad I missed it, you know?"

"Stuck your head in," I repeated.

"Yeah," said Hank. *"Went to look."*

"How did you know the painting was kept in the tower gallery? How did you know to call it that? Have you been to the Guggenheim before?" said Kat, narrowing her eyes.

"What is this, the third degree?" asked Hank. "My brother Ben, he works there sometimes. That's how I know all of this stuff. Anyways, the police and the fire department work closely together, so we get to hear a lot."

I remembered what Helen had said, that Ben had heard about Gloria being arrested from the firefighters. Now we had discovered that Hank and Ben did not just know each other—they were brothers. That was why I had recognized Hank's last name. I had heard it during the roll call. We thought we could rule out the fire crew, because they could not have been in the Guggenheim on Monday. But what if Ben and Hank were working together, just like Kat had suggested Lana and Helen might be? Brothers were even closer than friends, weren't they? Hank could not have ordered the moving van using Aunt Gloria's card, or dropped the smoke bombs, but maybe Ben could. Then, when Hank arrived in his fire engine, he could have stolen the painting. It was an interesting possibility. I was more excited than ever.

"Hank!" shouted someone from inside the station, where we could not see.

"Gotta go," said Hank, glancing behind him. "You kids clear off, OK? And hey—say hi to London when you go back there."

"We will," said Kat, nodding. I thought that she was lying again.

He turned away, and Salim raised his camera and took a picture of Hank's wide blue back next to the fire engine.

We walked away down the road, and when we came out at the end of it, I turned to Kat. "What if Hank and Ben were working together?" I asked.

"Yes, Ted, exactly!" said Kat. She punched me on the arm, but I didn't mind.

"And he told us more about the smoke bombs," said

Salim. "We know they're the kind used for paintballing. What if one of our suspects does paintballing?"

"That's not a clue!" said Kat. "It doesn't matter who does paintballing. You don't need to do paintballing to find out about something on the internet and order it."

Salim's face crumpled up. "Oh," he said. "You're right."

"But we're getting closer!" I said. "There are only a finite number of possibilities left."

"Finite!" repeated Kat. Her mouth went up at one side. "Ted, how did I get a brother like you?"

I opened my mouth to explain.

"Don't be LITERAL, Ted!" shrieked Kat. "I didn't mean TELL ME!"

Salim snorted, and put his hand over his mouth. "I really am glad you're here, Ted," he said.

Kat opened her notebook and scribbled in it again. We were narrowing down our suspect list. I remembered the equation I had imagined at the beginning of the mystery. We were looking for x, and it seemed as though we were coming close to discovering it.

30

SCYLLA AND CHARYBDIS

We came out on the northwest corner of Union Square. I noticed that the tilt of the earth and the position of the sun meant that its light was passing through more air to reach ground level in New York. Each air molecule it bumped against made it scatter more and more, so that by the time it reached our eyes, it was red and yellow instead of blue.

Kat raised her hands to her eyes. "Look at the sunset!" she said.

I tilted my neck back down to look at the city around us. The grassy square was to our right, with trees and paths and people jostling each other along them. Hot, dirty smells came up into my nose, and traffic flashed between us and the square, stopping and starting, a circuit breaking and coming together again. I noticed that the traffic was stopping more than it should, and people were leaning out of their cars and waving their hands as their horns blared. We turned through ninety degrees, and that was when I saw the reason for all the horns and shouting. Part of the street, the part under a green sign with white lettering that said UNION SQUARE WEST, was blocked off by bright orange traffic cones. Three people in bright orange suits were crouched around a hole in the ground. I wondered if it was a sinkhole that had opened up under Manhattan.

Salim put his camera up to his eye and took a picture of the men. Then Kat said, "Come on!" She grabbed Salim's arm and ran toward the men. I did not think Kat was being very sensible. She was not obeying the rules of the road, and that was dangerous.

"Kat!" I shouted at her, but that word was lost in the honking and other people's shouts. I squeezed my eyes shut and my hand shook itself out. Everything suddenly felt too loud. I felt like Odysseus again, Odysseus facing the whirlpool Charybdis.

I counted and breathed, and then I opened my eyes

again. I could do this. The orange DON'T WALK sign turned white and said WALK, so I walked, ten paces across the road, and came to where Kat and Salim were standing. They were both shouting at the men in orange jumpsuits, because one of them had picked up a heavy drill and was using it. It jolted across the asphalt, shooting noise out into the air.

"HELLO!" screamed Kat.

"BEN!" shouted Salim. "I KNEW YOU'D BE HERE!"

"SALIM!" shouted Ben. "HEY, GUYS, STOP!"

I looked at Ben and saw that his body was approximately the same size and shape as Hank's, and their faces had the same proportions. He also had freckles across his face and body. It was true: this was Ben, and he was Hank's brother.

The other men stopped drilling. Ben stepped toward us to talk to us, and turned to Salim. "Hey, guys. Salim, I heard your mom got arrested," he said. "I'm sorry."

"Yeah, but she didn't steal the painting," said Salim. "She didn't!" His eyes were suddenly shining. "Someone framed her."

"That's not what the police are saying," said Ben.

"Yeah, and that's what you told your brother, and now everyone thinks it's true," said Kat, folding her arms.

"We know all about Hank, by the way. You shouldn't have hidden him."

Ben's lips pressed together and turned down. He was puzzled. "Yeah, Hank's my brother. Salim, I told you about Hank!"

"You never told me what he did!"

"I'm telling you now," said Ben. "Hank's a fire-fighter. So?"

"He came to the Guggenheim yesterday," said Salim. "Why?"

"Total coincidence," said Ben, shrugging. "The Eighteenth Street crew was the nearest free crew when the alarms went off. Look, you coming here accusing us of something?"

"We . . . ," said Salim. "Um—all right, just tell us one thing. What were you doing on Monday?"

"Monday? I was in the Guggenheim that morning, fixing a pipe. Angie had an appointment that afternoon at three, so I left around two to take her there. Helen was there too, she saw me leave, and—yeah, I saw Lana when we got to the hospital. You know about her pop, right?"

I translated. In New York–speak, *pop* sometimes means dad. Ben's face was still puzzled, but there was another expression in it too. I could not work out what it was. This was frustrating.

"Oh," said Salim. "So you were at the hospital all afternoon?"

Ben nodded his head *yes*. "Look. I didn't have anything to do with what happened yesterday," he said. "When the smoke started, it came from right next to me, on the first floor. I got confused at first, went around in circles. Then Rafael ran down the side stairs and onto the main floor. He bumped right into me and we got out together. I didn't see anyone else."

This fitted the evidence of my eyes and, if it was true, ruled out both Ben and Rafael as the thief. But I still had questions.

"Who's Angie?" I asked. "And what was Lana doing in a hospital?"

"Angie's my wife," said Ben. "She's sick."

"Ted!" said Salim. "Look, I'll explain later."

"Salim, it's OK," said Ben. I kept on looking at his face. His mouth was turned down, and so were his eyes. I finally knew what I was seeing. This was sadness. "It's cancer. I have to take Angie for treatment. Lana visits the same hospital because of her pop. He's got Alzheimer's, you know? He's getting worse."

"We did not know," I said.

This was very important. I realized that this was the thing that Lana had not wanted to say to us—her father was ill. This meant that she had not been in the museum on Monday to steal the credit card from Aunt Gloria's purse and call the moving company.

I had one more important question that I needed to ask. "What's in the hole?" I asked.

"Ted!" said Salim.

"I'm sorry, he didn't mean that," Kat said to Ben.

"I did!" I said.

"Water pipes," said Ben shortly, his body turning away from us, back to the manhole.

The drilling started again.

"Oh, Ted!" hissed Kat. She and Salim were walking away from the hole, and so I had to follow them. "Why do you have to be so—*you*?"

"I can't be anyone else," I said once we were approximately five meters from the hole. I thought this was a reasonable statement. "But this means that Ben did not make the phone call. I think we can rule him and Hank out—if Ben was telling the truth about the hospital."

"He is," said Salim. "His wife's really ill. Ben's been trying to raise money to pay for her treatment."

"Why can't the National Health Service pay for it?" I asked.

"Shh, Ted!" hissed Kat. "Don't be stupid. There isn't an NHS in America."

"Everyone pays for their own medical treatment here," added Salim. "And treatment for cancer—well, that's expensive."

Even though we knew they could not have done it, this would have been a good motive for Ben and Hank: they needed money to help Ben's wife. They are family, and family means that you do things for each other, even when you are different, like me and Mum and Kat and Dad. We have the same genes, and that is important. It means that we are connected.

I was so busy thinking about DNA, and feeling sad that we had ruled out Hank and Ben when they had such a good motive, that I forgot to wait for the light. I stepped out into the street, Kat screamed behind me and something *screeeeech*ed on one side of me. I spun round and saw the yellow nose of a taxi almost against my leg in its gray trousers.

There was more noise and I looked up to see a woman waving her fist. She had climbed out of the car and was leaning forward, her face screwed up and red. She was very angry.

"*What the heck are you doing, kid?*" she screamed, except she used a swear word when she said it. I guessed that, because she said *kid,* she was talking about me.

My hand began to flap. I did not want to be talking to this woman. "Hrumm," I said. My throat felt full and my heart was beating very fast.

"What's wrong with you?" screamed the woman. "Look at me when I talk to you! I almost hit you! I coulda dented the car! Whatcha gotta say?"

My head went to the side. I turned back to Kat, but that meant I was looking straight into the sun. It burned a red streak into my eyes. I couldn't see Kat and Salim. The woman was shouting and shouting. In *The Odyssey,* for his most difficult task, Odysseus had to sail between Scylla—a six-headed sea monster—and the whirlpool Charybdis. This was the next test on my quest, but I was not ready for it. Odysseus faced Scylla, but I didn't want to.

I ran forward, across the road and into the Union Square subway station.

31

WRONG TRAIN

I was trying to get back to Aunt Gloria's apartment. Kat doesn't believe me when I tell her this, but it's true. I haven't had enough practice at lying, and anyway this would be a useless lie. I wanted to be as close to Mum as I could, and shut myself in Salim's room and jump on his bed in circles. I had had enough of adventures and quests.

I saw the number 6 of the subway in glowing green above my head, and I knew that was a train that would take me there. I went toward the sign, and that was when things went wrong.

I am a dyslexic geographer. I have problems understanding left and right. I followed the sign down a set of gray concrete stairs that smelled like the toilets at school. I had my subway card in my pocket, and I took it out and fed it into the turnstile, then shoved through and onto the platform. The train came screaming out of the black tunnel, two points of light and then a blur of silver. I got on it. I was breathing very hard and my hand kept shaking itself out. I did not notice that the train I had got on was going the wrong way.

Then I saw that the numbers were wrong. They were leading me away from the apartment. I closed my eyes and opened them again, but it was still true. I was on the wrong train, in the wrong city, and I did not know what to do.

"Young man," said the white woman sitting next to me, pushing her face up close to mine. She had a big nose, and pearls on a string round her neck, and her face was sunken in on itself so I could see all her bones. She was very old. "Young man. Are you lost?"

"Yes," I said.

"Young man," said the woman. "Look at me. Where is your family?"

I shrugged.

"You're not from New York, are you?" she asked. Her

breath smelled like mints and wet coats. "No. You're a tourist. I can tell. And you've gotten yourself separated from your family. Where is home?"

"Rivington Street, in London," I said.

"Well," said the old woman, "that isn't particularly helpful to us today. Where is your family?"

"I don't know," I said, because that was the truth.

"Let me see. What about Times Square?"

"What about Times Square?" I asked.

"It's where most tourists end up," said the old woman. "You ought to go there. Even if your family isn't there, the information center will be. They'll be able to help you get home. You're a capable young man, aren't you? You can manage that."

One and a half minutes earlier, I would have disagreed with that statement. But hearing the old woman say those words had made them feel correct. That is the way spells work in *The Odyssey*. Someone says something, and it becomes the truth. And it *was* true. I *had* wanted to go to Times Square, and the old woman had reminded me of that.

"I can manage that," I repeated.

"Good," said the old woman. "Now get out here, and follow the signs to the N train. It's the yellow one. Go north, and get out at Forty-Second Street. The information center is on Forty-Fourth."

The doors of the train opened. The woman flapped her hands at me. "Go on," she said loudly.

So I stepped out. I was in a station I didn't know, surrounded by people who were all rushing past me. But then I realized that if I followed them, they would probably take me where I needed to go. So I went down a long corridor that led to a line that was yellow. The people around me shoved my body onto the train and I was carried seven stops. Then the doors of the train swished open, and a voice said, "Forty-Second Street—Times Square." I remembered what the old woman had said. It was time for me to get out.

32

ALL THE LIGHTS IN THE SKY

I was outside, in air that was heavy and warm and made my skin feel tight. It was almost night, and the buildings around me were tall and dark, but the signs hanging from them were bright, flashing every color.

People were talking and music was playing and there was so much light, as though all of what was vanishing from the sky was being poured into Times Square. On the building in front of me, a long thin golden french fry dipped into a tub of ketchup, over and over again. Below that a red neon guitar played itself, but no sound came out. A drink poured out of a can into a red cup, again and again. There was a black sign that said HEROES in huge white letters. The *O* was a total eclipse, with the moon in front of the sun, but there was a spot of light at the top right of the moon where the sun was coming out again. That was me, I thought. By getting myself to Times Square on my own, I was being a hero, just like Odysseus.

I knew that the old woman had told me to look for Kat and Salim in the information center, but instead I stood and looked and looked. I realized that if I looked up past the people, with my hands over my ears to block out the noise, all I could see were the patterns of the neon signs. The panic I had felt earlier was gone. I was calm.

As I stared at the billboards, at squares and circles and lines blooming in blue and yellow and red, I realized that they were a bit like the missing painting. They were shapes hanging on a wall as well. Were they priceless too? And if not, what was the difference?

I was still trying to understand why *In the Black Square* had been stolen, and now I had time to think. And for some reason what I thought about were hands.

I saw Salim's hands taking a photograph of Helen and Lana in the square garden.

Kat's hand reaching out to touch Salim's arm.

Aunt Gloria's fingers covering her eyes as she cried.

My hands putting my Magnum chocolate into Ty's palms.

Mum's hands on my back as she rushed us out of the Guggenheim.

I imagined another hand, Vasily Kandinsky's, painting colors onto his canvas almost one hundred years ago. Did he matter more than these billboards, and if so, why? Was it because he was dead? Would Salim's photographs, and all these signs, be priceless one day, just because the people who had made them were dead too?

And then I thought about the hands that must have dropped the smoke bombs into the Guggenheim space and pulled *In the Black Square* off the Guggenheim's wall. What did those hands look like? And what had they done with the painting?

33

RED AND WHITE AND BLUE, PART TWO

I watched the drink pour into the cup forty-seven times while I thought. Then someone put their hand on my shoulder.

This was the eighth time someone had banged against me. I imagined that my molecules and the other person's molecules had touched each other for a moment before they bounced away into the rest of the universe. But this time the person did not move away. Instead, they pulled me round toward them.

I was staring at a sparkly shirt that I knew, and hair chopped into a shaggy cut. Kat's face was red and patchy, and her eyes were small with tears.

Her mouth opened wide, and then she was scream-ing into my face, "WHAT IS WRONG WITH YOU, TED SPARK?"

That was an easy question to answer. I am bad at di-rections. But I suspected that was not the answer Kat wanted, so I didn't say anything.

Kat burst into tears, and threw her arms round my shoulders. I stared at the red-and-white patterns of light falling on her hair. I saw that Salim was standing behind her, clutching his camera.

"Kat," I said. "Salim. Thank you for coming to find me." I meant it so much that my throat hurt.

"Oh, Ted, I thought I'd lost you!" said Kat. Tears went spilling out of her eyes again, and her mouth wobbled. "But then I thought about the subway sta-tion, and I realized that you'd gone the wrong way. When you didn't come back to Auntie Glo's apart-ment, I just had a *feeling* that you'd ended up here. I thought you'd like the lights. And I remembered how you said . . ."

Salim had put his phone up to his ear. "We've found him," he said. "He's in Times Square, just like we thought. Aunt Faith, it's all right. Tell Mum to stop cry-ing. I can hear her. *Mum!*"

"Are we going back to Aunt Gloria's apartment now?" I asked. "Has Aunt Gloria been released by the police?"

"Um, Ted. No," said Kat. "Auntie Glo's still being questioned. We had to call Mum and Auntie Glo when you went missing, and they are totally going to kill you next time they see you. You know they thought you'd pulled a Salim? Actually, they were already upset because Sandra told them that we weren't there this morning when she came to look after us. She's been searching for us all day. She found me and Salim when we went back to look for you, and she made us go back out to keep hunting. I mean, she didn't really *make* us—I would have come anyway."

"I know you would, Kat," I said.

"Ugh, yes, whatever," said Kat, her lips twisting. "You are so *annoying!*"

I didn't think that Kat meant what she said. I also thought the part about Mum and Aunt Gloria killing me was a figure of speech. I did not want to be killed before we could solve the Guggenheim Mystery. I felt as though what I had thought about in Times Square had been useful. I could not explain it, even to myself, but I was sure that I had had a very important idea.

*   *   *

189

Salim made another phone call, to Sandra. Five minutes later, a police car came screeching up to us, making Times Square light up even more in red and white and blue. Sandra jumped out of it.

Screeching was a good word to use, and not even a figure of speech, because when Sandra came toward us, her blond hair was down from her bun again and she was shouting.

"HOW DARE YOU!" she cried. "I've wasted *all day* looking for you!"

Sandra was a very small person, but at that moment she frightened me. I backed away from her.

"What did you think you were doing?" snapped Sandra.

I remembered that we had to keep our quest a secret. "I went the wrong way on the subway. I'm sorry," I said. "We were just being tourists. I wanted to see New York."

That was my sixth lie, but Sandra didn't know that. She breathed deeply through her nose and smoothed down her skirt with her hands. Then she was calm. I couldn't see anger on her face anymore at all.

"All right," she said. "Get into the car. I'm taking you all back to my apartment."

The policeman had got out of the car and was standing in the road next to it, speaking into his walkie-talkie. It had a red light glowing on it, which meant that someone was speaking back.

"Situation under control," he said. "Final missing child located."

That was strange to hear. I realized that for a few hours we really *had* been missing, just like Salim last spring.

Kat was holding Salim's phone up to her ear. *"Mum!"* she said. "Didn't I tell you? We're fine, honestly! We promise we'll be good."

Mum should know by now that when Kat says *honestly*, 87 percent of the time she is not being honest. I have conducted careful research on this.

Then we got into the police car. Sandra sat in the front, with the officer, and Kat and Salim and I were in the back.

I observed how strange police cars are. They have a grille that separates the back seat from the driver, in case a criminal tries to attack them. I sat still and imagined that I was not a hero anymore, but a criminal. I wondered if this was how Aunt Gloria had felt when the police arrested her.

I was still wondering this when the police car arrived at Sandra's apartment.

34
SANDRA'S PAINTINGS

I asked Kat why we couldn't go back to Aunt Gloria's white apartment. Kat said, "The police are still searching it, Ted!" I imagined police officers going through the rest of my suitcase, looking at my encyclopedia and unfolding my underwear as they hunted for clues. It felt as though they were turning me inside out. I remembered when Salim disappeared. Then the police had felt sorry for us, and Aunt Gloria had been the victim. Now they thought she was a criminal.

Sandra's apartment wasn't far from Aunt Gloria's. It was on Ninety-Fourth Street, in another tall building with fire escapes climbing up its outside. Looking at them still made me feel dizzy, as though I was seeing something I shouldn't be able to. It was like I had X-ray eyes, and I was seeing through the bricks of the building to its skeleton. This is a simile, but an interesting one.

We climbed up five flights of stairs, Salim dragging his feet. Sandra waited for us at the top of the stairs.

"Come in," she said. Her face was calm again, and as Salim walked past her she patted him on the shoulder.

We stepped through Sandra's doorway, and I saw that her apartment was even smaller than Aunt Gloria's, with the same living room–kitchen space. Its walls were white too, but they were covered with bright-colored pictures. For a moment my heart beat irregularly because I recognized them—they were some of the paintings that I had seen in the Guggenheim. What were they doing here?

"Oh!" said Kat. She had seen them as well.

"You have paintings from the Guggenheim on your walls!" I said to Sandra.

"Of course I do. Those are *prints*," said Sandra. "I could never afford original paintings, so I collect these instead. They're not the same as paintings."

I went up to one of the prints, the picture of the green woman floating on a red background, and squinted my eyes at it. Close up, the colors looked flat. When I moved my head, I could not see brushstrokes. I touched it and felt glossy paper. So it *was* just a photograph of a painting, not the painting itself. I looked around at Sandra's walls.

"You do not have any Kandinskys," I said.

"No," said Sandra. "I told you, I don't like them. Seurat and Chagall are more my taste."

My taste is another way of saying *my preference*. None of the prints on Sandra's wall looked like *In the Black Square* at all—so she had been telling the truth yesterday. Sandra liked art, but she didn't like Kandinsky.

"How many copies of paintings are there?" I said to Sandra.

"In the world?" asked Sandra, and her eyebrows went up. "Millions, I should think. These are only worth a couple dollars each."

So value was like an equation. If there is one of something, it is worth millions of pounds. If there are millions of something, each one is worth two dollars, which is equal to one pound. So Sandra owned—I looked around the room—approximately twenty dollars' worth of art.

"Salim," I said, "you should sell your photos. If you only printed one copy of each one, you'd make lots of money."

"Yeah, sure, Ted," said Salim. He turned away from me.

"Leave it, Ted," said Kat to me. I did not understand what I had done. I'd wanted to cheer up Salim, but it hadn't worked.

Sandra was nice to us. She let us watch her TV (although she made us watch a channel that I was not interested in), and she kept bringing Salim herbal teas, which he didn't drink. Then she cooked dinner for us, which was steamed fish and steamed vegetables. This proved that she was not used to having children in her apartment. Kat made faces and moved her plate aside. Salim ate without looking at his fork. I created a circuit on my plate, broccoli touching zucchini touching carrot touching limp white fish.

"Sandra," said Kat. "Have you heard from Auntie Glo? Is she all right?"

"I don't know anything more than you do," said Sandra. "It's a terrible thing. In all of my years as a gallery assistant, I've never seen anything like it. It's shocking."

"Mum didn't do it!" said Salim. This was the first thing he had said for thirty-seven minutes.

"Of course, that's what we all hope the police will decide," said Sandra.

"But someone used her credit card!" I said. "They

stole it on Monday. She's being framed. How will the police find that out?"

Kat kicked me under the table. I don't know why—I was telling the truth. I wanted Sandra to say the same thing to the police so they would let Aunt Gloria go.

"I was there on Monday, Ted," said Sandra. "I was in and out all day, but I didn't see anyone steal anything from Gloria's bag. You need to leave the detecting to the police."

No one spoke again for the rest of the meal. After that it was time for bed. Salim and I were going to be in Sandra's guest bedroom. Kat was going to sleep on the floor in Sandra's room. Kat opened her mouth to argue, but Sandra said, "That's what's happening, Katherine, like it or not," and that was that. Kat scowled, and went stomping off to the bathroom to change. She didn't even point out to Sandra that Kat is short for Katrina, not Katherine. I thought that if she could shut Kat up, Sandra must be good at telling people what to do.

I put on the pajamas that had been brought from Aunt Gloria's apartment, and then stood outside the bathroom. Everything felt wrong to me.

"Ted!" said Sandra, folding her arms. "Move it!"

I moved it. I went rushing into the bathroom and

locked the door. Then I climbed into the bathtub and pressed my face into the tiled corner, where the two walls met. I breathed in and out four times and then I thumped the wall. Sandra shouted something and knocked on the outside of the bathroom door, so I timed my thumps to hers.

After a while her thumping stopped. I thumped twenty-nine more times, because 29 is a prime number, and then I got out of the bathtub and opened the door. Sandra had gone away, but Kat was sitting in the hallway, waiting for me.

"Ted," she said, and she pointed to the floor next to her. I sat down. "Ted, I know it's awful, but you've got to be good," she whispered. "You can't upset her."

"I'm sorry, Kat," I said.

"I know," said Kat. "Ted—I love you. I'm sorry I shouted at you earlier."

I was surprised that Kat was still thinking about that. "I love you too, sis," I said.

Kat's eyes went shiny. "Good night, Ted," she said, and she jumped up and went running into the bathroom, because I had been in it for a very long time.

35

STEALING THE SCREAM

I lay down in Sandra's guest room next to Salim.

"Salim," I said. "I can hear you breathing irregularly. You aren't asleep."

"Ted," said Salim. My hypothesis that he was awake had been proved correct. "Do you ever stop being a detective?"

I thought about this. "No," I said. "It's just the way my brain works. Are you upset about Aunt Gloria?"

"Yes, Ted," said Salim. "She's my mum! And I'm worried. I don't know if we can help her."

"It is not a certainty," I agreed. "However, it is also not impossible."

"You're so weird, Ted," said Salim. "If anyone else said that, it'd sound awful. That's why I like you."

"I like you too, Salim," I said. "We're friends."

"We are," said Salim.

"Salim," I said. "I am going to get up and do some more thinking about the case."

I went into the living room. I wanted to read my encyclopedia. I wanted to know everything it said about paintings, and people who stole them. But I couldn't, because it was still at Aunt Gloria's. So instead I looked at Sandra's books.

She had a big bookcase that was full of books about art. She even had some about art theft. I looked at a book called *Great Art Heists from History*. It was a big hardback. I had to balance it on the kitchen table because it was so heavy. I found out that of all the art stolen, only 5 to 10 percent of it is ever recovered (the lower number was the one that Aunt Gloria had used earlier, proving that although she is imprecise, sometimes she is still correct about things). Usually the thieves have some connection to the gallery or museum the art is stolen from. Most people steal art because it is worth so much money. There is a *black market* (which means a secret group, not lots of stalls painted black) of criminals who want to buy it. Sometimes they want to use it to trade for other illegal things. Sometimes they just want to ransom the painting for lots of money—if the museum leaves a bagful of money under a bridge, or in a dustbin, the painting will be returned. And sometimes they just want to look at it, to have a painting hang in their house forever. I thought about this idea—that someone might have stolen *In the Black Square* because they liked it.

I made a list in my head of all the reasons why someone might have stolen *In the Black Square*. The list looked like this:

1. To sell it for money to someone they hadn't met yet
2. To sell it for money to someone who already wanted to buy it
3. To ransom the Guggenheim (This did not seem very likely, since we hadn't heard about any ransom note)
4. To trade it for something else they needed, such as medicine for Ben's ill wife, or Lana's ill father
5. Because they wanted to look at it (This

would rule out Sandra all over again,
because she did not like Kandinskys)

I found out that the worst art thieves in the last hundred years were the Nazis. They stole paintings from all the cities they invaded, because their leader, Adolf Hitler, wanted his own museum to be full of his favorite art. They even took paintings from the Jewish people they killed. Thinking about that made me feel ill. I stopped reading that chapter.

Some of the most famous paintings in the world have been stolen. In 1911 the *Mona Lisa* was stolen from the Louvre Museum in France by a man who'd previously worked there, and in 1994 *The Scream* was stolen from a museum in Oslo.

The Scream is an extremely interesting painting. It is a picture painted in bright, frightening colors of a man screaming beside a blue sea and a red sunset. At least, that is what it looks like. But that is not really what the painting is about. The man is not actually screaming—he is *hearing* a scream from outside the frame of the painting. His mouth is open because he is afraid of the sound coming from all around him. The painter, Edvard Munch, is playing a trick on everyone who looks at the painting, and he does it because people see what they expect to see.

The biggest art theft in history went down on March 18, 1990. It happened at the Isabella Stewart Gardner Museum in Boston, USA. The thieves, disguised as policemen, stole thirteen objects, which were worth a total of $500 million, including a painting by Rembrandt called *Christ in the Storm on the Sea of Galilee*. It is a picture of Jesus calming the waves during a storm, which is something that is factually impossible, but it is very famous and the police have been trying to get it back ever since. There is still a reward of $5 million to anyone who can find it, which made me think that I should look for that painting as well as *In the Black Square*. It would solve all Mum and Dad's money problems, and mean that there was enough left for Kat to go to fashion school.

But *In the Black Square* was still the painting I had to find first. And I did not know how to do that. I sighed, and my hand shook itself out, and that was when Kat came creeping into the living room.

"Kat," I said. "You're creeping."

"*Shhhh!*" said Kat. Her shoulders were hunched over, and she was walking on her toes, like a burglar.

"What are you doing?" I asked.

"*I can't sleep,*" hissed Kat. "What are *you* doing?"

"I'm reading about why people steal paintings," I told her. I explained what I had discovered.

Kat narrowed her eyes. "Interesting, Ted," she said. "That reminds me. We haven't looked at our suspect list together since we talked to Hank and Ben. Look, I've re-written it so we can see all our latest clues." She went over to her backpack and pulled out her notebook.

WHO COULD HAVE STOLEN THE PAINTING?

1. Lionel. (Security guard. The second-to-last person to leave the museum. Because he is the security guard, he must know how to shut down the burglar alarms and security cameras, and we know they were down yesterday morning.) Problem: Could he have made his voice sound like a woman's to trick Effortless Light Moving? And was he at the Guggenheim on Monday?

2. Helen. (Head of the maintenance crew. Third last.) Was fixing fountain at the Guggenheim on

Monday, so had opportunity to steal the credit card and call Effortless. Says she doesn't have a motive, but she hates Gloria. Lied about the fact that she was with Lana during the smoke.

3. Lana. (Member of the maintenance crew. Third person out of the museum after us.) Left very close to when we did. She would not say what she was doing on Monday—now we know that she was visiting her ill father in hospital. She could not have made the call, but she might be working with Helen.

4. Rafael. (Janitor. Came first out of the museum after us. He was also with Ben.) Ben seems to have given him an alibi, but we need to make sure it is true.

5. The builder, Gabriel. (This is very unlikely. He was working on the outside of the building, and never went inside. Although he might have climbed in through the broken skylight to steal the painting. This is Ted's idea. We need to test it to see if it is possible.) Gabriel was also late to the roll call, which is suspicious.

WHO HAS BEEN RULED OUT?

*Aunt Gloria (because she is being framed), Sandra
(because she is too small to have carried the
painting, and also she was wearing very high heels),
the fire crew (because none of them could have been
at the Guggenheim on Monday), Ty (because he was
not near the museum on Monday afternoon), Jacob
(because he could not pretend to be a woman on
the telephone; also, his eyesight is too bad for him
to have been able to carry the painting through the
museum, and he was at his granddaughter's concert,
so he has an alibi for Monday afternoon), Hank and
Ben (because neither of them could have made the
phone call to Effortless, although they need money).*

"Ted," said Kat, sitting back in her chair. "There are two suspects we haven't spoken to yet, and one crucial place we need to go that we haven't gone."

"The Guggenheim," I said.

"Exactly," said Kat. "We have to go back into the museum."

"Sandra will probably go there tomorrow," I said. I used the word *probably* because tomorrow was a Saturday. This meant I couldn't be sure, but I thought that there was at least a 51 percent probability that Sandra would go to work even on a weekend.

"*Exactly,*" said Kat. "All we need to do tomorrow morning is make sure that she takes us to work with her. Since we ran away yesterday, I bet she will—she'll want us to be in a place where she can watch us. And that also puts us in the perfect position to solve the mystery!"

36

BACK IN THE GUGGENHEIM

Breakfast the next morning was bread that was gray and full of pieces.

"It's gluten-free," said Salim, poking it. Sandra was in the shower, and she had told us to have finished breakfast before she got out of it. "Mum eats it sometimes too, when she's on one of her diets."

"It's repulsive," said Kat. She was wearing her tight jeans and the same sparkly shirt she had worn yesterday. "Ugh! Why doesn't anyone have Hovis in this country?"

"And Shreddies," I agreed.

"Oh, poor Ted!" said Kat, looking at me. "I forgot— you hardly ate anything yesterday. Mum's going to *kill* me!" She was being Big Sister Kat, worried about my health. She pulled open the big white fridge, which glowed on her face and arms, and dug through it. Then she closed it again and went through the cupboards until she came out with a banana, which she waved at me. "You can eat this," she said. "A banana is a banana, wherever you are."

It looked bigger and more yellow than London bananas, but I cut it up into exactly seven pieces, with the two ends left on my plate, and ate it in seven careful bites.

I felt better after that.

Then Salim went digging in the fridge and came out with a bright-colored box, opened at one end. "Pop-Tarts!" he said. "I *knew* Sandra wasn't into health foods as much as she pretended to be!"

He put three into something flat and hot called a *toaster oven*—two for him and one for Kat (they were pink and white and covered in sprinkles, and I didn't want one), and he was halfway through his second when Sandra came into the kitchen, patting her hair, which was done up in its bun again.

"Salim!" she said in a voice that was very high. She didn't like what he was doing, and I deduced that this was because she was embarrassed about having something so sugary in her kitchen, the way Mum gets when we find her chocolate hidden in the empty flour tin.

"Caught you!" said Salim, sprinkles jumping on his lips as he spoke. "You hide Pop-Tarts in your fridge!"

"Oh!" said Sandra. She lifted her lips in a smile. Her cheeks had turned pink. "Yes, you caught me out, Salim! Now, are you ready to go? I'm not leaving you here all day, after what you did yesterday."

"Yes, Sandra," said Salim.

"Yes, Sandra," said Kat, and behind Sandra's back she winked at me.

"Good," said Sandra, and she went rushing out of the kitchen. Salim and Kat slapped palms again. I knew they were pleased that we were going to the Guggenheim without even having to beg Sandra. We were very lucky that morning. I don't usually believe in luck, because it is unquantifiable, but that is what we were.

I was ready to leave, dressed in my school uniform. I was secretly glad that no one had reminded me to put on new underwear. Although New York kept changing, my clothes stayed the same.

* * *

The policeman on the forecourt of the Guggenheim, guarding the white-and-blue police tape, let us through because we were with Sandra. The museum was still closed because of the theft. Then Lionel, yawning but still smiling at Salim, waved us through the main revolving door, which was being kept open for the police, and we were back inside the Guggenheim. I was worried about Lionel. He was one of our remaining suspects. He seemed nice, but what if he was not?

At least the museum was quiet again. All the hoovering and hammering and buzzing had stopped. The main rotunda was empty, just ten open crates standing there on the floor. The white walls of the Guggenheim were empty too, and its ramp was clean.

"All right," said Sandra, turning to Salim. "I need to spend a few hours in the office. I've got a call with the director—he's flying home from Beijing this afternoon, and he wants to know the latest before he takes off. Then, at one p.m., Lieutenant Leigh is coming by to talk about the case. Lionel can look after you, but *don't* disturb me, please."

"Yes, Sandra," said Salim, nodding his head.

"Sandra," said Lionel from his seat next to the door, "I'm not sure I should be watching them."

"Lionel, will you please do your job for once?" snapped Sandra. *Snapped* is a word that in this case means she spoke fast and loud, her lips pursing up.

Lionel raised his palms up in front of his chest and widened his eyes. "All right, Sandra," he said. "Go."

Sandra walked away to the triangular stairs, her high heels clipping on the stone floor.

"Yowch," whispered Lionel when Sandra had walked out of our sight. "What bit her today? Apart from the usual, I mean."

"Well," said Salim. "We . . . kind of ran away yesterday. She spent the day looking for us. She even called the police."

"Salim!" said Lionel. "Your mom must have been going crazy!" Then he looked sorry. I guessed that he was remembering where Aunt Gloria was at the moment. "Look, you're having a hard time. I'm not going to yell at you. Do what you want this morning. Just stay quiet, and don't make Sandra mad at you. Deal?"

"Deal," said Salim. "Thanks, Lionel."

Lionel smiled at him. I was still worried. Was I reading his emotions correctly?

"Hey, Lionel!" said Salim. "One more thing. Were you here on Monday afternoon?"

"Monday?" asked Lionel. "Huh. Yeah, I was. I've been working extra shifts lately. Why?"

"No reason," said Salim. "Don't worry!"

Lionel shrugged and then went back to his seat. I saw him breathe out heavily as he sat down.

But I was very relieved that Lionel wasn't paying attention to us anymore. We were going to be left alone, and this was good because we had detective work to do, and we were finally in the right place to do it. We could go and see where the painting had hung, and see if it helped us work out how the thief might have taken it.

First, we were going to climb the Guggenheim ramp. We hadn't been able to do this on Thursday, because it had been full of the maintenance crew, but now it was empty, so we could. I had been wanting to do this since I had first read about it. I was excited.

We started at the bottom and began to climb up. The light falling from the black-and-white skylight at the top of the Guggenheim was calm and pale, and the strips of light that lit the ramps from the triangular light fixtures above (or below, depending on how you look at each level) were soft on the empty walls. That morning the lights on the second and third levels were still off, though, because no one had been back in to fix anything since the painting had been stolen.

I remembered that the lights were a very interesting thing about the Guggenheim. When it was first built, there were no lights in the plans. Frank Lloyd Wright thought that all light should be natural, and did not include lights in his original design, but after he died, they were added.

All the paint on the ramp walls was new, the brush-strokes reaching the very edges of the bank of triangular light fixtures. I sniffed, and I could smell it, and also smell the ghost of the smoke in the air. It made my good feeling falter. I also saw where the police had been: the marks of their feet on the floor that had not been cleaned yet, and the police tape stretched across the tower gallery from which *In the Black Square* had been stolen.

As I walked upward, the sweep of the Guggenheim wrapped around me. Salim and Kat stopped on the third floor and hung over the edge, shoulders pressed against each other, whispering and pointing, but I carried on, all the way to the top, where I looked up at the big black-and-white skylight and saw the one shattered pane showing the real blue of the sky. Then I turned and walked down again. I looked at the shiny stone surface of the floor as I walked, and saw myself mirrored dimly in it: two Teds, one light and one shadow. I circled round, through six complete rotations, or 2,160 degrees, and then came down again onto the rotunda floor. I walked up and down three more times, and I felt calmer than I had been for days. My head was full of circles, and that helped me see something that I should have seen before.

I came up behind Salim and Kat.

"I know what's wrong with the way the painting went missing," I said to them.

37

WHICHEVER WAY YOU LOOK AT IT

They both jumped. I realized that I had made my voice too loud.

"Look!" I said, trying to be more quiet. I pointed down at the packing crates on the rotunda floor. "I should have noticed it as soon as we came in. They've been moved around since the day the painting was stolen, and opened, but there are still ten of them, just like there were on Thursday. None of them are missing."

"So?" asked Kat, raising her eyebrows.

"Which crate did the thief put the painting in?" I asked. "We know that Effortless Light Moving carried a crate out of the museum's loading bay on Thursday morning. So we thought that the thief must have put the painting in one of these crates and taken it to the back entrance. We thought that was how the thief stole the painting. But we don't *know* that. It's just a theory. And I've realized that it's wrong. I remember that there were ten crates when we first arrived on Thursday, and there are still ten this morning."

"Ted!" said Kat. "Oh my—you're incredible!"

"Wait," said Salim. "Yeah, but—what if the crate was already waiting in the loading bay? Maybe we've just been wrong about which crate the thief used? They might have just carried the painting through the museum and packed it up in a crate that was already there."

"Oh! That could be it," said Kat. "That would still work. Except—hold on. How long would that take? We've been saying that the people who came out earlier had less chance to steal the painting, but we don't know yet exactly how long they'd need."

"The alarm went off at ten-twenty-one a.m.," I said. "Sarah said that the van was booked for ten-forty, but she also said that the driver arrived a bit earlier than he was meant to. This is anecdotal evidence, but it is believable because it was backed up by Billy. He said that it came at ten-thirty-four, remember? That is thirteen minutes after the alarm went off. So the painting must have been in the loading bay by then."

"Wait, Ted!" said Kat. She was flicking through her notebook. "Look at this! The van came at ten-thirty-four. But the fire engine only came at ten-thirty-two. If it takes more than two minutes to get from the tower gallery to the loading bay, then we're totally right—there's no way Hank could have stolen the painting, or any of the fire crew. Salim, how can we work out how long it takes to go from the second-floor tower gallery all the way to the loading bay?"

"Er," said Salim, "you'd need a museum pass to get to the loading bay. Only staff and crew can go there. I sometimes borrow Mum's pass, but I don't have it now."

"Well, we've got a staff member right here," said Kat. "Why don't we ask him?" She pointed down at Lionel.

"Wait!" I said. "What if Lionel is the thief? He will not want us reenacting the crime."

Salim frowned. "That's true, Ted," he said. "Um—OK, we don't have to tell him what we're doing. I'll say we're playing a game, all right? He'll believe me. He trusts me."

I wasn't sure, but I didn't know what else to say to stop Salim. Kat and I leaned forward on the edge of the ramp and watched as Salim ran down to where Lionel was, and he and Lionel talked. Lionel shrugged and handed a flat card to Salim. Salim came running back up to us, beaming.

"Easy!" he said. "Lionel's way too nice. We just have to get it back to him by his lunch break."

"Right!" said Kat. "Let's do this. Salim, go to the door of the second-floor gallery, where the painting was taken from. Ted and I will stay up here on the ramp so we can watch. Ted, when I say *go*, you start timing with that fancy watch of yours, and Salim, you walk from the gallery to the loading bay, then come back into the main space and go out of the main entrance. Remember that when you're going to the loading bay you need to walk, not run, like you're carrying a huge painting and it's really smoky so you can't see properly. Ready?"

Salim nodded. I nodded. I was excited. I was also glad that the cameras were still down, so Lionel couldn't see exactly what we were doing from his position at the Guggenheim main door.

Salim ran down the ramp of the Guggenheim and then in through the doorway of the tower gallery, below us. Kat and I watched him get into position.

"GO!" shouted Kat. I pressed the timer button on my weather watch, and after thirty seconds Salim came walking out of the tower gallery again, his arms stretched out and his feet shuffling, like he was holding a big painting. Salim, I thought, was a very good actor.

He shuffled carefully down the triangular stairs, and then opened a door and went hobbling through it. I looked at my weather watch. Five minutes and five seconds had passed.

Two minutes and thirty-two seconds later, Salim came back through the door, this time running instead of shuffling, and went out of the main entrance. I looked down at my weather watch.

"Seven minutes and fifty seconds," I said to Kat.

Kat's lips turned down.

"Auntie Glo came out of the Guggenheim after seven minutes," she said. "That's what you told us, Ted. And she was the last person out. Is there any other way the thief could have done it?"

I thought. "The ramp would take even longer," I said. "The distances are even further."

"But if even Auntie Glo didn't have time to do it—" said Kat.

"Then the method we thought was used to steal the painting is impossible," I said.

38

OCCAM'S RAZOR

There is a theory called Occam's razor, which says that the simplest explanation is true. I have read about it in my encyclopedia, but I had not connected it to this case until now. Taking the missing painting all the way to the back door of the Guggenheim while the building was full of smoke was not a very simple or easy thing to do. So what if they had done something else instead?

"Could the thief have left an *empty crate* in the loading bay earlier that morning for the van to pick up, to make us and the police think that the painting was inside it?" asked Salim. "And then—they might have hidden the painting somewhere else? It's misdirection! Right, Ted?"

I nodded. *Misdirection* is something that Salim, as a practical joker, understands. So do I. It is what magicians use to make you look the wrong way when they are doing a trick. It is always something that is meant to catch your eye, like a bright red scarf or a white rabbit—or a moving van.

"And that's why there wasn't just one moving van, but *two!*" said Salim. "Effortless Light Moving, then Elephant Moving. I've been wondering about that. It didn't make sense. But it does if they're meant to keep the police chasing the wrong lead for ages. Of course!"

Both Kat's and Salim's eyes were wide, and Kat was jumping up and down on her toes.

"The one thing we know for sure is that the painting is gone," I said. "So if the crate and the van weren't used, there are . . . four possibilities for how the painting was taken out of the museum."

I was thinking quickly. I was excited, because I was looking at the case in a new way. I counted my ideas off on my fingers on my left hand: thumb, index, middle, ring. I kept my right-hand fingers tucked into my right palm.

"*One,* the painting was taken out from above, through the broken skylight and down the scaffolding. *Two,* it was hidden somewhere for a while, somewhere the police didn't see it, then taken out of the back entrance, but later than we have been thinking—after the van left. *Three*, it was taken out of the front entrance, but we didn't see it leave. *Four*, it spontaneously combusted."

"Te-ed!" groaned Kat. She had taken out the notebook from her backpack and had been scribbling my thoughts into it as I spoke. "It isn't *four*. Stop saying that! Come on! It's got to be one of the other possibilities. If it was *one*, it must have been Gabriel the builder."

"Gabriel *and* someone from the museum," said Salim. "Because we still know that the thief took Mum's credit card out of her purse to book the vans. Mum's card was in her office, behind a secure door, and Gabriel doesn't have a museum pass, so that means someone else would have needed to be involved. OK, so it's at least eight feet from the ramp to the skylight. If someone stood below it and held up the picture, then someone else could lean down and pull it through."

Eight feet is 2.44 meters, or 244 centimeters. The painting was 97.5 centimeters by 93.3 centimeters, without considering the frame. The shortest person working in the Guggenheim was Lana, who (using empirical evidence) I estimated to be 1.62 meters, or five feet and four inches. If you add her height to *In the Black Square*'s, you make 259.5 centimeters, which is enough. Lionel was taller, five feet and nine inches or 1.75 meters. Both of these heights were definitely *plausible,* which means possible.

"What if Gabriel is the answer?" Kat asked. "What if the thief stole the painting, ran back up to the top of the ramp and passed it out to Gabriel? It could be! We have to go outside *now* and question him. This could be it!"

39

ONE

Kat went storming out of the main door. (*Storming* is a figure of speech that means walking quickly and angrily. I like it very much.)

"Wait!" said Lionel. "Where are you going? Give me back my pass!"

But Kat ignored him. She rushed past the policeman, who looked at us when we went by but didn't try to stop us, to the bottom of the grid of scaffolding that covered the Guggenheim. I had not liked the scaffolding when I first saw it, but now I realized that I did like the way its metal poles were held together to make squares. It looked so solid, but it could be folded away into nothing but lines.

Then Kat began to wave her arms and jump up and down. "HEY!" she yelled upward. A very little stick figure stuck its head over the side of the fourth level of boxes. It was wearing a hard hat and orange coveralls.

"WHAT?" he shouted back down.

"WE NEED TO TALK TO YOU, GABRIEL!" Kat screamed, her earrings and her hair flying as she moved. Her fingers bunched up into her palms and then burst outward, as though her hands were dancing. Salim took a picture of her, the corners of his mouth turning up as he put the camera to his eye. I thought I would like to see how Salim saw Kat at that moment.

"WHAT DO YOU WANT WITH ME?" yelled Gabriel, taking off his sunglasses.

"COME DOWN AND WE'LL TELL YOU!" shouted Salim.

This seemed to work. Gabriel came swinging down the scaffolding and landed on the ground, his big arms folded. He put his glasses up on his helmet and I saw that his cheek below his eye was stained with a bruise.

"We want to ask you about Thursday," said Salim. "When the smoke alarm went off, you were late for the roll call, and we want to know why."

"Why is it any of your business?" asked Gabriel.

"Because," said Salim. "Er—"

"Because," said Kat firmly, "Salim's mum's been arrested for stealing that painting. We know she didn't do it, because we know her, so we're trying to find out who else might have taken it. *And . . .* you were on top of the Guggenheim, so you might have looked through the skylight and seen what was happening inside."

Kat was being clever, I realized. She was not accusing Gabriel of stealing *In the Black Square.* She was behaving as though we only thought he might be a witness.

"I didn't see anything," said Gabriel. "Why would I? Kid, as soon as the alarm sounded, I got off the scaffolding. Ask any of the tourists who were there."

"Yeah, but . . . ," said Kat. Then she spoke fast. "Yeah, but my brother saw you coming to join everyone outside the museum later. Where had you been?"

"I'm not answering that," said Gabriel, very quickly. "No way. It's got nothing to do with you."

That was when Salim's brain began to work properly again. "Please," he said suddenly. "I've got to know what happened. My mum's going to be put in prison. *Please* help."

Gabriel scowled. "Look," he said. "I've got nothing to do with this. Yeah, I was late for the roll call, but it

226

didn't have anything to do with the robbery. Swear up and down."

I imagined a swear word moving up and down. It was a strange thought.

"Look. Just before the alarm went off, I got a call from my, uh, ex-friend. He heard that I, uh, had a new, uh, friend, and he was, uh, mad at me."

Gabriel's face had turned red, and he was looking away from us, down at the ground. This meant that he was embarrassed about what he was saying—or was he lying? I couldn't tell.

"Anyway, like I said, he was mad, and he came here to argue with me. I climbed off the scaffolding to Eighty-Eighth Street to calm him down—and when I got back, everyone was outside the museum and Gloria was taking roll call."

"How do we know you're telling the truth?" asked Kat. This was a good question. Gabriel's story definitely seemed *shady* to me.

"This!" said Gabriel. He pointed to the bruise on his face. "I got it during our talk. He hit me, all right? Now leave it!" he said angrily. "That's the truth. I wasn't up on the scaffolding, so I didn't see anything. And I was with, uh, my ex-friend until I came out to the roll call, so I couldn't have stolen any painting. I'm going back to work now. And look—don't tell anyone else about this, all right?"

"All right," said Kat at once.

Gabriel turned and swung himself back up onto the scaffolding.

I looked at Kat. She looked at me. She shook her head. I knew I was missing important information, but I also knew what Kat was telling me: that whatever the reason for Gabriel's red face, his bruise meant that he had not stolen *In the Black Square*. It was an empirical fact. I remembered seeing him rubbing his face and yawning when he joined the roll call. I had thought he was tired, but now I realized that he was rubbing his face and moving his jaw because he had just been hit.

"Kat, why are you so sure that Gabriel wasn't lying?" I asked.

"Because of his story," said Kat. "He's gay. All that stuff about friends? He meant *boy*friends. It was his ex-*boy*friend who came to argue with him. That's why he looked strange. He was worried we'd judge him."

I thought about this. One of Kat's friends is a boy, and has a boyfriend. He is not embarrassed about it at all, because it is no different than a girl having a boyfriend

(Kat explained this to me), but I knew that some adults haven't been told this properly.

"Boyfriends shouldn't hit you!" I said, concerned.

"You're right, Ted. Gabriel's ex-boyfriend is a horrible person. But he still gave Gabriel an alibi. Gabriel couldn't have stolen the painting."

Kat was right. And I came to a conclusion. Gabriel had not had anything to do with the robbery. There was no other way the painting could have gone out of the skylight without someone noticing, and so we could cross *one* off our list.

40

WHICH DOOR?

We had two possibilities left. I imagined them as my fingers, index and middle.

Index, *two*, was *taken out of the back entrance, but after the van left.*

Middle, *three*, was *taken out of the front entrance, but we didn't see it leave.*

"What about the loading bay?" said Kat. She had drawn a heavy line through one, *out of the window.* "And if it was taken out that way, does that change our suspects?"

I thought about this. "It still has to be someone who had access to the Guggenheim offices, and who could have stolen Aunt Gloria's credit card and called the moving company on Monday," I said. "That's Lionel and Helen and Sandra. Ben, Hank, Lana, Ty and Jacob couldn't have done it."

"But it still has to be someone who could have carried that heavy painting," said Kat, nodding. "So Sandra's still out."

Then I had an idea. It had to do with the loading bay. "If we're investigating *two*, we have to go talk to Billy again!" I said.

Kat wrinkled up her face. "We've already spoken to him," she said.

"Yes, but I think Billy might be a person who only answers the questions you ask him!" I said. "Like me. We didn't ask him if he saw *anything* that *day*. We asked him if he saw any *vans* that *morning*."

"Ted's right!" said Kat. She was whirling, her hands flying, her eyes shining. "Come *on*!"

We ran past the policeman again, and up to Eighty-Ninth Street. Billy was sitting exactly where we had left him, under the sign that read NATIONAL ACADEMY MUSEUM. He was still wearing green trousers and a blue shirt, and the shirt still had two buttons missing. The only difference I could see was that the cardboard he was sitting on said AID RAISI instead of UN-MAID R. This meant that he had moved, although not by much.

"Salim!" shouted Billy when he saw us. His mouth opened and I saw his missing incisor again.

"Billy, we've got to ask you something," said Salim. He was panting, and his camera thumped on his chest.

"What happened to your tooth?" I asked, because it was something I wanted to know.

"Swallowed it," said Billy. "Ate an apple wrong, and it went down into my stomach. Never saw it again. But it's still there. Did you know that teeth sit in your body for years? They don't move."

I did not think this was true.

"That's *not* what we wanted to ask," hissed Kat, jabbing me with her elbow. "We wanted to know—*after* you saw the van stop and the driver pick up that crate, the day the painting was stolen. Did you see anyone going into the Guggenheim by the back entrance? Or coming out again? Holding something?"

Billy nodded, flicking through his notebook. "The police," he said. "There was a guard on the back door from eleven-fifteen a.m. A van from Ultimate Security

Cameras at two-twenty p.m. And a guy in a blue uniform, with the Guggenheim logo on the shoulder, earlier. Tall black guy. Round face. Kinda heavy. He carried something out at ten-fifty a.m. and came back ten minutes later. After the alarms went off, but before the police turned up."

"Lionel!" said Kat and Salim together.

"Where did he go?" asked Salim, his voice wobbling up and down. This meant that he was upset. Even though Lionel was one of our remaining suspects, he was Salim's friend. "And what was he carrying?"

"Down Eighty-Ninth to his car," said Billy. "Blue Toyota Corolla. He was carrying a box. Medium size, brown cardboard, kinda this big."

My heart sped up. Then he waved with his hands, about forty centimeters apart. I was confused. This could not be the painting. It was not big enough. But if not, what was it? What had Lionel wanted to take out of the museum before the police arrived?

41

THE OPPOSITE OF A PANOPTICON

"Why didn't you tell us that before?" shouted Kat.

"Calm down, girlie," said Billy. "You didn't *ask* about people, just vans. How was I supposed to know you wanted to know about the people too?"

"This is it!" said Kat. "This is *it*!"

I was not sure. The box Lionel had been carrying was the wrong size to be the painting, after all. And what about the van that Billy had mentioned that afternoon, from Ultimate Security Cameras? Did that have anything to do with the mystery?

"We have to go and see Lionel!" said Kat.

"Hey," said Salim. "Billy—thanks, man, you've been amazing. We've got to go."

"Anytime, Salim," said Billy, grinning.

As we ran away from Billy, back toward the Guggenheim, Salim's phone beeped. He looked at it. "It's Ty," he said. "Wants to know if we've cracked the case yet."

"I mean—Lionel's one of our last suspects," said Kat. "He's the security guard, and so no one would have wondered why he was walking out of the back entrance. He did go around the museum on Thursday morning, remember? That could have been his opportunity."

I was very interested in what she had said about no one noticing Lionel. It is true that most people only see things when they aren't normal. They can walk down a street and not see that there are ten men and twelve women and five children on it, and that the third building along has three windows on the first floor and a tree in front of it that sticks out of the pavement one meter from the shop front and is encircled by twenty-seven thin gray bricks. They only notice when something is odd or out of place, like someone wearing a flamingo hat.

A security guard walking around and in and out of the building that he is guarding is like three windows in the third building—nothing is broken or funny or wrong, and so to most people it is invisible.

I was thinking this as we walked back through the Guggenheim entrance. Lionel wasn't at his usual place. He was halfway up the ramp, staring around the Guggenheim as though he was trying to watch all of it at once.

The technical term for a place from where you can watch everything at once is a panopticon. Usually Lionel's guard station would have been a panopticon, but now that the cameras were down, it wasn't. And then I remembered what Billy had said about the Ultimate Security Cameras van arriving at 2:20 p.m. Thursday, and the two memories stuck together in my head and turned into one big conclusion.

"Hello!" called Lionel, waving at us, and then he hurried down the ramp until he was standing in front of us.

"Hello," I said to him. "You didn't call the security company until after the painting had been stolen and the police had arrived, even though you must have known on Thursday morning that the cameras and alarms were not working."

The skin on Lionel's face turned grayish.

He took two steps backward and moved his hand from his stomach to his heart. "Listen, I never said . . ."

His eyes went to the camera above us, and then down to his stomach. I couldn't see how those two things were connected.

Kat's eyes narrowed. She stepped forward. *"Did you tell the police that you knew the cameras weren't working?"* she asked, sticking out her chin.

Lionel held up his hands and sighed. "Yeah, I did," he said. "I had to, as soon as they arrived. They would have asked to see the tape at some point. Some of the cameras went out on Tuesday afternoon. I thought that they'd just been knocked out by the crew when they came in to start work on the new exhibition. And usually it doesn't matter. If people *see* the cameras and the alarms on the wall, they think they're on. It's enough of a deterrent."

"Which ones aren't working?" asked Salim. His eyes had gone very narrow. I saw that his hands were shaking against the strap of his camera, where it looped down onto his chest. He was angry because he knew that if the cameras had been on and the alarms had been working, the police would already have been able to work out who the real thief was, and Aunt Gloria would not be in trouble.

"The whole left side. That means the cameras and alarms on this side of the rotunda, as well as in the tower:

the gift shop, the side galleries, the café, the stairwells and the loading bay," said Lionel. "This place—it's always breaking, and everything needs a special fix. Floors crack, you've gotta call the crew. Lights go out, you've gotta call the crew. Cameras and alarms, you've gotta get someone from the security company. And I did. Well . . . I called them Thursday morning, but they couldn't get here till later. Till after the painting was stolen. When the director finds out that I didn't call them in on Tuesday, I'm gonna be fired, and I *can't* be fired. I've got kids to look after." His mouth went down. He was upset.

"My mum's been arrested!" said Salim.

"I know," said Lionel. "Salim, I'm sorry. Believe me."

"*Salim,*" said Kat. She put her arm round Salim. Salim swayed and opened his mouth without saying anything.

"We were just talking to someone who was outside the Guggenheim on Thursday," said Kat, her chin sticking out once more. "And they said that they saw you going out of the loading bay with a box just before the police put up a cordon around it, and then coming back ten minutes later. Why did you leave the museum?"

Lionel's body twitched. His hands clenched. "That's— that was nothing to do with the robbery," he said very quickly. "I just had to put something in the car. Something for my kids. Don't—that's nothing to do with the painting, all right? Look, I've gotta go. I need to talk to—I need . . ."

And he hurried away without finishing his sentence.

I thought this was unusual behavior. I also did not believe that he was telling the truth about what the box had been, or when he had called the security company. Lionel was lying—why?

42

ANOTHER DEDUCTIVE PROBLEM

"I think Lionel was lying about calling the security company!" said Kat, once he had gone.

I was pleased, because Kat had made the same deduction that I had.

"But the box he was carrying wasn't the right size to be the painting!" said Salim. "And . . . well, it just can't be Lionel. He's—he's nice. I like him."

I thought that Salim should be more rational. But I also knew that there was one other possibility.

"If it was *three,* if the painting was taken out through the front entrance of the Guggenheim, it *could* still be someone else," I said.

"What if Hank from the fire crew hid the painting in his uniform?" asked Salim.

This was not a good deduction. I shook my head. "If the painting is too big to be in Lionel's box, then it is too big to be hidden in a uniform," I said.

How things fit in space is a language that I understand. I held my arms out in front of myself, approximately a meter apart. "Look, it's nearly *that* big. It's wider than a person. It is longer than their legs, even most tall people's legs."

"But it's thin if you turn it sideways," said Salim. "What if the fire crew had a ladder? What if Hank draped some material across the ladder and hid the painting under it?"

"It could be!" said Kat, her eyes widening.

"The fire crew didn't take in a ladder," I said. I remembered this.

"How do you know?" said Salim. "They might have!"

"They didn't," said Kat, sighing. "Ted knows."

Kat was right. I knew. My memory would have a ladder in it if there had been one.

But remembering the ladder also made me realize something else, even more important. There was still something wrong with how we were thinking about the mystery. The world was full of possibilities, but there was one fact destroying each one.

The painting was too big.

It was too big for *any* of our theories to fit, now that the idea about the painting being put into a crate had gone. It couldn't have been lifted out of the skylight, or taken out of the back door later on, or out of the front door, without anyone noticing. It was too big for that.

So the thing that I had to change in my mind, and in all our theories, was *In the Black Square*'s size.

I had to find a way to make it compress down into something smaller, and once I had done that, I would be able to see how the thief had stolen it. I imagined the big square of the painting folded up seven times (which is the maximum number of times you can fold an object as large as this painting).

I shook my head, frustrated. It was a stupid thought, because I knew that if the thief had folded up the painting, that would damage it, and that would mean it wouldn't be worth as much money anymore. Besides, the painting had a wooden frame, and you can't fold up a frame.

But then I realized that, once again, I had been thinking in the wrong way. We had been imagining what was stolen as a large square, just like its title: the painting with its big frame, about a meter wide and a meter high. But what if we were wrong?

What if the thief had cut the painting *out of* the frame? What if they had taken the square frame and broken it down, the way scaffolding breaks down, and hidden the pieces somewhere?

A picture did not *need* to be framed. What if we were not looking for a square at all, but a rolled-up piece of canvas?

I was very excited.

"If it was rolled up, it *could* have been hidden in the museum!" I said. "We might have a fifth theory!"

43

INSIDE OUT

I said that. Then I looked around. The curl of the Guggenheim around me was smooth. There were no cupboards, no floorboards, no corners. There were side galleries, but they had all been checked. The police had been here on Thursday—they would have found it when they searched. There was nowhere to hide a painting, not even a rolled-up one. Another possibility exploded into billions of atoms of air.

"Wait!" said Kat, waving her arms. "What did Helen say, about working on fake walls? What if it's hidden behind one of those?"

We all looked at each other. Then we went running up

the ramp, toward the place where Helen and Lana had been working.

A plywood wall had been built in front of the real wall so that a big painting could be hung on it. Kat scrabbled at it with her hands and stuck her head through the narrow gap between the fake wall and the real one. Then she stuck one of her arms in and waggled it around.

"Anything?" asked Salim.

Kat made a noise. "*Urk!*" she said. "Hold on . . . there's something . . . !" She wriggled back out of the wall, her face very red. "Look!" She had something in her hand, a gray plastic packet done up with tape. "It's too small to be the painting!" she said, her mouth turning down and her forehead wrinkling. "It feels . . . knobbly."

"Open it!" said Salim.

Kat scrabbled at the tape and the packet came open. Nails came pouring out, all over the shiny ramp floor.

"What on earth . . . ?" asked Kat. I didn't know. This was very strange. How did this fit into the Guggenheim Mystery?

Kat pulled out eight more packets, four with screws or washers in them instead of nails, three with screwdrivers and other tools and one with hammers of different sizes.

"I don't understand," said Salim. "There's no painting in there!"

Kat shook her head.

I turned and stared around at the Guggenheim. Smooth white walls. Smooth stone floor. Smooth white ceilings and smooth white light fixtures.

Salim's shoulders went down.

"Wait!" said Kat, sitting back on her heels. "I know! What about the offices in the tower? You said there are lots of them. Anyone could hide some rolled-up paper in a pile of papers!"

This was a good deduction from Kat. I was impressed.

But Salim still didn't look cheerful. He shook his head again. "It's a paperless office," he said.

I imagined an office with no papers, the printers whirring, people opening empty paper file after empty paper file.

"*Paperless office* means that everything is stored on computers," Salim explained. "It's meant to be better for the environment, but it's stupid, 'cause Mum can never find anything she needs. She keeps a box of printouts at home."

So my imagining had been right. I was pleased with myself.

"So?" said Kat, sticking out her chin. "Come on! Don't give up! Even paperless offices have *cupboards,* don't they?"

Salim just shrugged. He was thinking something, but I could not deduce what it was. He led us down the ramp to the main floor, and we went up the triangular stairs again. I looked up and saw triangular lights, the same shape as the long banks of lights winding up the ramps, but individual triangles instead of an unbroken line. It reminded me of Times Square, with all the lights together.

We went up five flights of stairs, past the gallery and the café (Salim went in and dug through the drawers behind the counter, but there was nothing inside them but a few bags of pasta), and then Salim waved Lionel's pass against a panel in the wall and pushed open a door.

And I understood why he had not been cheerful.

44

LITERALLY PAPERLESS

We were staring at a bright white box with wide, white-framed windows and a white-tiled floor. There were six desks with six white computers balanced on them and gray chairs tucked underneath. There was a very small white set of drawers next to each chair, and on the desk nearest to us were two books and three plastic folders. There was a label that said GLORIA McCLOUD. That was all I could see, and I knew that my eyes were not lying. There was nowhere to hide a meter-long painting and its frame in this room—even if the painting was rolled up and the frame was broken into pieces.

A smooth blond head of hair rose up from behind the

computer at the desk opposite Aunt Gloria's. Sandra was staring at us.

"What are you doing here?" she asked.

"I was just taking them on a tour," said Salim.

"Didn't I tell you not to bother me?" asked Sandra. "Go away! I'm just off the phone with the director, and now I'm preparing for my meeting with Lieutenant Leigh. I don't have time." Her eyes narrowed. "Why isn't Lionel with you?"

We left before she could ask us anything else.

"They're all like that," said Salim in a low voice when we were back out on the stairs. "Both floors of offices. I didn't want to say anything, but . . . it's impossible. The café's all open as well, like you saw. There's so little space to store things that they're always running out of food. I know you don't want to believe it, but there's no way that the painting could still be in the museum."

Then I heard a sound below us. It was a low hum. It was the sound of a hoover—and there had been a hoover vacuuming at the Guggenheim just before the robbery.

"Kat!" I said. "Salim! The hoover!"

Salim looked as though he didn't understand me, but Kat's eyes widened. "Salim!" she said. "We still haven't spoken to Rafael. I bet that's him!"

* * *

We went running down the stairs again. The triangles made me dizzy, and I bumped my shoulder against the stone wall. I was going to keep running, but then Kat caught my arm and pulled me to the right, and then right again. I saw that she had brought me into the second-floor tower gallery, from where *In the Black Square* had been stolen. The blue-and-white police tape was still across the place where the painting had been, but there was a man in the middle of the floor, spinning a large machine in circles.

The man turned and saw us. He was medium height, with lots of curly black hair and big, bushy eyebrows, and he had brown skin. He was wearing a navy-blue jumpsuit with the Guggenheim Museum's logo sewn on it in white on his shoulder. This was definitely Rafael, who had come out with Ben the day the Guggenheim was robbed.

"Rafael!" said Salim. "It's you! We heard someone cleaning."

"Salim, hey!" said Rafael. "I heard about your mom. I'm sorry."

Salim's face tightened and his jaw clenched. "She didn't do it," he said. "She was framed."

Rafael held up his hands. "All I'm saying is what I've heard," he said. "She's been arrested, hasn't she? That's what Sandra told me when she called me to come in today."

"Yes, but . . . it wasn't Mum!" said Salim. "Look, did you see anything on Thursday? Anything that might help her?"

"I didn't see anything," said Rafael. "But, man, it was awful, wasn't it? As soon as the smoke started up, I got out. Left the vacuum cleaner in the third-floor gallery, went running straight down the side stairs. I came out on the first floor and ran into Ben. Knocked him over. It would've been funny if, you know, we hadn't been afraid we might die. We got up and ran out together."

Kat nudged me. I knew what she meant. Rafael's and Ben's stories fitted together.

"I almost didn't come back today, but like I said, Sandra told me to. This place's gotta be cleaned, now that the police have been through it. They left footprints everywhere!"

Salim nodded at him. "Thanks," he said.

"I need to ask you one more question," I said. "Were you here on Monday?"

"Monday?" asked Rafael. "Nope. Had to call in sick. Got a stomach bug, and I was throwing up all day. My mom looked after me. Why?"

"It's not important," I said. It was not. Rafael had been ruled out as well.

He turned away, back to his machine, and as he started to spin it across the floor, Salim took a photograph.

45

SPINNING IN CIRCLES

Rafael spun his way out of the tower gallery, and we were left alone in its square white space, facing the empty place on the far wall where *In the Black Square* should have been. But the painting was not there. The probability of it being somewhere else in the universe was 100 percent, and that was good in a way, because at least it was certain.

I looked around the rest of the gallery. It was filled with paintings, large and bright and strange. Why had *In the Black Square* been stolen instead of one of them? It was not worth more than the rest of them. It was worth millions of pounds, but they were too. And it was not as big, or as colorful, as some of them. I wondered if it was true, what I had been thinking about at Sandra's—that the thief had stolen the Kandinsky because they liked it and thought it was special.

There was one particular painting that my eyes saw. It was only circles on a dark background that looked cloudy, as though someone had spilled water across it. The circles were blues and yellows and reds, and they overlapped each other like the primary-color tests Miss Woodfine, our art teacher, had made us do in year 4. *Blue and red make purple, blue and yellow make green.*

When I mixed the colors, though, all I got was brown. I looked it up in my encyclopedia, and found that when you mix paints together, the more you add, the darker everything goes. Blue and red and yellow make black. But when you mix *light* instead of paint, blue and red and green (green is a primary color for light, not yellow) make a white light. This is because white light is not really white at all—it's made up of all the visible frequencies of light in exactly the right balance.

I liked that idea, and when I looked at that painting, I wondered whether Kandinsky, who had painted this as well as *In the Black Square,* had heard about white light too. I thought he had. The circles looked as though they were getting paler, not darker, the more they overlapped.

I stared at the painting, which was called *Several Circles*. Salim said, "That's worth thirty million dollars, you know."

Kat gasped and said, "No way!"

"*Why?*" I asked.

Salim understood. I knew he would. "Because there's only one of it in the world," he said. "Because millions of people want it, but it can only be in one place at a time."

"And because it's *beautiful*," said Kat. "It's exciting. It makes me feel—stretched. I want to do that when I make clothes."

I stared at the circles of the painting. For a moment I understood what Kat meant. Looking at that painting was like trying to understand something new. It was Kandinsky's special code, like *In the Black Square* had been.

"I thought I hated modern art before Mum got this job," said Salim. "But it's not so bad, really. At least it's not horses in fields and people on swings. I look at some old paintings and I know that those posh white people would hate me. I'd be a servant, right? Or I'd be the person the soldiers were fighting. But circles and lines and colors aren't like that. They're—I don't know—open."

"Yes," I agreed. But I was still thinking about these paintings, and comparing them to the posters in the gift shop downstairs. I said this to Salim.

"That's just photography," said Salim. "That's not real art, not really."

"It so is!" said Kat.

"Do you think?" asked Salim. "But, Ted, the difference is the paint. When you go up to a real painting, you can see all the time the painter has spent on it. A photographic print is a different thing."

"But what about forgeries?" I asked. "They're paint."

"Ted!" said Kat. "Stop asking questions! It's not relevant."

"Forgeries aren't the right kind of real," said Salim. "Mum says that a painting is a piece of the artist's soul."

I translated this from Aunt Gloria–speak, and realized that she was saying the same thing that I had been thinking. You can't copy a brain. It is special. I had to think about the stolen painting as a part of Kandinsky's brain. It was important to find who had taken the painting because it would help Aunt Gloria. But I saw for the first time that it was also important because it wasn't just a thing that had been lost. It was a part of a person.

"It doesn't seem possible," said Kat, staring at the blank space on the wall under the security camera. "How *can* it have been taken?" She pulled out the notebook with the flowers on it. She held her tiger-striped pen over our new theories. "We might as well get rid of Ted's latest theory," she said. She pressed down with her finger, and the black dot of the pen squeezed down on the page. Then the pen—and Kat's finger—paused.

"*Copies,*" she said. "*Photographs.*"

I wondered if Kat wanted us to say something, but I stayed quiet, because I couldn't see what the next word in the pattern she was making would be.

"Er, Kat?" asked Salim.

Kat's head jerked up, and she stared at him. But even though her eyes were pointing at his face, they were looking somewhere very far away. "Salim," she said. "*Ted!* I've just thought of something. I think—oh my God—I think I know where the painting is!"

46

PRICELESS

"Where?" asked Salim.

"Come on!" shouted Kat, stuffing the pen and the notebook into her backpack and running toward the door of the gallery. Salim looked at me, and shrugged with his shoulders. I shrugged back, copying him. Salim began to run too, so I ran after him.

The echo of Kat running down the triangular side stairs bounced up to my ears. Salim and I followed her noise, moving through the air she had just disturbed as though we were planets being pulled in by her gravity. I felt again that I was on a quest, an adventure, just like Odysseus.

When we came back out into the main rotunda space,

I thought Kat had gone out of the main doors, and I wondered how she had done it without Lionel seeing. But then Salim turned right before we reached the main entrance, and I saw that we were in a new room. In here the lights were off, and the white walls looked cool and gray. I looked up and saw into the second-floor tower gallery, from which the painting had gone missing, and above that into the café. Then I looked to my left, where there were big clean windows. I could see a smooth gray strip of concrete, and then a dark gray strip of street, and then a green strip of park and finally a blue strip of sky. I imagined that I was looking at a painting in two dimensions, but then a yellow New York taxi drove from right to left along the road and I knew I was looking at the real world.

We were in the gift shop.

I remembered then that when the Guggenheim was first built, there wasn't a gift shop in the blueprints, any more than there were lights. Frank Lloyd Wright had wanted where we were standing to be a place where cars could drive straight up to the front door, because he wanted the Guggenheim to be a museum that moved as fast as New York. But, once again, Frank Lloyd Wright's plan had to change.

Then I looked right, at the room we were in. It smelled

expensive—of perfume and lemon cleaning fluid and paint. There were three large wooden cases, full of pens and pencils and games. I saw a bowl of wooden pens with small wooden Guggenheims on the end of them, a Rubik's Cube and a game where you can match colors to create different patterns. I thought Kandinsky would probably have liked that. Usually in gift shops there are clear plastic spinning racks full of postcards, but in this one the postcard holders were on the walls, and they were made of wood and glass. The rest of the walls were fitted with wooden drawers, and inside them were glass cases full of sculptures and jewelry. There were photographic prints of the paintings from the galleries upstairs on the wall too, and a set of drawers below them. Kat was crouching in front of these drawers, pulling each of them open in turn, so hard that they thumped at the end of their tracks.

"Kat!" said Salim. "Hey, Kat!"

"What?" said Kat. *Thump. Thump.*

"What are you doing?" asked Salim.

"Finding"—*thump*—"the"—*thump*—"picture!" said Kat, and then all the drawers were open, and she was scrabbling inside, pulling out long rolled-up tubes. These are how prints of paintings are stored, in gift shops. If you like a painting very much when you visit an exhibition, you can come here to buy yourself a copy to take home.

"Kat," I said reasonably.

Kat began to pop open the plastic top at the end of each of the tubes and pull out the posters inside. Green and red and black and white and yellow pictures scattered across her lap.

"Those aren't real paintings, Kat. They aren't worth anything. Salim just told us."

"EXACTLY!" shrieked Kat. "They *aren't* worth anything. They *aren't* the real pictures. You *said*! And then I thought—if I was going to hide something that was worth millions and millions of pounds, why wouldn't I hide it with all its copies? Who'd ever think to look in the gift shop?"

"You, Kat," I said, because that was a question with an obvious answer.

"Yes, me, but—come on, Ted, this could be it! Help me look!"

"Kat, you're amazing," said Salim, and he bent down to wrap his arms around her.

I knelt down and began to open tubes. I made a careful pile of pictures in front of me, and tubes behind me, and I observed two things. First, that what Kat had suggested was possible. Some of the prints were one meter square, or even larger. Some of them were even prints of *In the Black Square*. But my other observation was that none of the tubes I opened held the real *In the Black Square*. All the pictures were on shiny photographic paper, and they all had small printed letters in the corner that said GUGGENHEIM MUSEUM. I opened fifty-eight tubes and this never stopped being true.

I looked at Kat and Salim, and saw their faces crumple up, their mouths flatten, their eyes narrow. The probability of the painting being in the gift shop dropped to 10 percent, then 2 percent, and finally, as Kat opened the last tube, which was empty, it sank to absolute zero.

And that was when Lionel walked into the gift shop.

47

DEAD ENDS

"What are you guys doing here?" he asked, smiling. Then he saw the prints on the floor, and he stopped smiling. "Hey, what are you *doing*?" he said, much more loudly. "Pick those up!"

"We're looking for the painting," said Kat.

"The *painting* is miles away by now," said Lionel, not smiling at all. "We all know that. Come on, put those back!"

He stood over us until we had rolled up each of the prints and put them back in their tubes. I enjoyed myself. It felt like we were making a circular pattern. We had taken all the pictures out, and now we were putting them all back again. There was one empty tube left over when we had put all the tubes back in their drawers. I put it with the others in the top drawer.

I looked at Salim. His shoulders were very low, and his mouth was tilted down. When people want to say that someone is upset, they say *his face fell.* I always imagine a face dropping from its neck and landing on the pavement. At this moment, though, I realized that Salim's face looked as though it wanted to do that. So the figure of speech was not a figure of speech at all. I understood how much it had hurt Salim that we had not found the picture.

"Lionel," said Kat. Her lips were set in a very thin line. I thought she was about to do something potentially risky.

"What's up?" asked Lionel.

"What's up," said Kat, "is that you *still* haven't explained why you came out of the back of the Guggenheim just after the robbery, carrying a box. And we think you were lying about when you called the security company. You didn't call them until after the painting was stolen, did you? Why should we trust you? How do we know *you* didn't steal the painting?"

Lionel's face was scrunched up and his mouth was

open. "I don't—I didn't—listen, I swear that what that guy saw had *nothing* to do with the painting. Nothing!" He was standing over us, and he was so tall that he blocked out the Guggenheim's light, as though he was the moon during a solar eclipse, and we were on earth trying to stare at the sun, or as though I was Odysseus, and he was the Cyclops. "Look. You're right. I didn't call the security company until eleven, after the painting was gone. But that's not because I stole the painting. It's because of the box I was carrying out to my car, and *that* has nothing to do with *In the Black Square*. I'll tell you, but you've gotta promise me you won't tell anyone."

"All right," said Salim.

"All right," said Kat.

Then I felt something jab into the space between my ribs. It was Kat's tiger-striped pen, and I realized that Kat was communicating with me without words. She was telling me that she was lying, and that I should lie as well.

I coughed. "Yes," I said. "We will do that. Not tell anyone. Yes." That was my seventh lie. They were getting easier.

Lionel rubbed his hands across his face. I did not breathe. Then he said, "OK. That box . . . that box had food in it. Not some stupid painting. I've been going up to the café and taking supplies. Nothing they'll notice—just cans of tomatoes, bags of pasta."

I remembered what Salim had said earlier, about the café running out of food, and thought that Lionel wasn't correct when he said that no one would notice the food he was taking. Someone *had* noticed: Salim. He had just not understood what it meant.

"I do it a lot. I take the boxes down the stairwell and leave them in the loading bay until I'm finished with my shift. I'm security, so no one ever asks what I'm doing. I do it every time the cameras break.

"But then, when the smoke happened and the police were on their way—man, I knew I had to get the latest box out before they arrived. I knew they'd notice it and ask me questions. That's what I was doing when that guy saw me—taking the box to my car. I swear, it was nothing to do with the painting."

Salim's face twisted up. "You stole from the Guggenheim because you wanted some food?" he asked.

"Yeah," said Lionel. I noticed that his face was flushed and his voice was shaking. "Do you know what I get paid? And do you know what the rent is, even in Brooklyn? My wife died a couple of years ago. It's just me and my kids now. So, yeah, I do what I can." His shoulders lifted in a shrug.

Now I understood why Lionel had looked at his stomach before, and why he had stared up at the ceiling. He hadn't been thinking about the painting—he had been thinking about the café, and food. This is why it's very hard to deduce what people are imagining just by watching their bodies and faces. So Lionel was not a suspect anymore. We could rule him out.

And that meant the only suspects left were Helen Wu and Lana, working as a team. By logical deduction we had solved the Guggenheim Mystery. So why did it still seem unfinished? We did not know why they had hidden the tools behind the false wall. We did not know where the painting was, or how it had been taken out of the museum. We were still confused.

Salim's phone beeped. "It's Ty," he said. "The maintenance crew has been called back in."

Then Lionel's walkie-talkie crackled. "Security, come in," said Sandra's voice.

"Security here," said Lionel. "What's up?"

"Go find the kids and tell them to get themselves an ice cream or something. I don't want them here when the detective arrives."

"Sure, whatever you say," said Lionel. "I'm with them now. Got that, guys?"

"Whatever," said Salim, shrugging.

"They got that," said Lionel into his walkie-talkie.

Salim took a picture of Lionel in the gift shop, the poster tubes behind him and his walkie-talkie in his hand. Then Lionel clipped the walkie-talkie back on his belt and put his arms round Salim.

"It'll be all right, kid," he said. "I promise."

But Salim pulled back from his hug. "Come on, Ted, Kat. Let's go."

As we followed him out of the museum, my brain waves were spinning. How could we solve the Guggenheim Mystery now?

48

OUT OF THE BLUE

We sat on the hot white steps of the Metropolitan Museum of Art, which is also on Fifth Avenue, and ate ice cream. I had another Magnum. I gave the chocolate to Kat, but she was eating something called a Creamsicle, which was bright orange and fizzy, and she waved my hand away. So I gave it to Salim. He was eating a Good Humor bar, which I thought was a bad name, both for it and Salim. Salim was not in a good humor. He stared at the chocolate from my Magnum and let it melt down his fingers. I stared at it too, and thought.

"We need to be logical," I said. "There are people we have ruled out. It can't be Jacob, because he wasn't in the museum on Monday to steal Aunt Gloria's credit card. It can't be Ty, for the same reason. It can't be Sandra, because she is too small and couldn't have carried the painting anywhere, and she couldn't have smashed the frame with her high-heeled shoes. It can't be Gabriel, because he didn't have a pass for Aunt Gloria's office, and also he was busy arguing with his friend. It can't be Lionel, because he was committing a crime, but not the right crime. He is a thief of food, not a thief of art. Unless he was lying to us?"

I said this because I was still not sure I knew when people were lying. Lionel's guilt or innocence rested on the way he behaved, and that wasn't something I could be certain I understood. I knew that I was sad at the thought that Lionel might be fired, but that wasn't useful for my deductions.

"He was telling the truth," said Salim. "I know it, just like I knew he was lying before. I know him."

"Hrumm," I said. "All right. We also know that it wasn't Ben or Rafael, because they ran into each other very soon after the smoke started, and gave each other alibis. Rafael and Ben were also not at the museum on Monday. It wasn't Hank, for the same reason. That leaves Helen and Lana. We know that Lana lied about being with Helen when the smoke happened. We know that Lana wasn't at the Guggenheim when Aunt Gloria's card was stolen, and she could not have called the moving companies either, but Helen could. We know that Lana needs money because of her father being ill, we know that Helen and Lana are friends and like working together, and we know that Helen does not like Aunt Gloria, so wouldn't mind framing her. We found things hidden in the Guggenheim near where they were working—which might be a clue to how they smuggled out the painting."

"That's good, Ted. That's really good! But if we just tell the police it's them, they won't believe us," said Salim.

"They might!" said Kat. "We've got lots of evidence!"

"We haven't," said Salim. "Because we still don't know where the painting is or how they stole it."

Kat sighed and her lips turned down. "Unless we can show the police the painting and prove Auntie Glo didn't steal it, then you're right. None of it matters."

"Excuse me," said a lady from two steps above us.

Kat took another bite of her Creamsicle. Orange covered her lips.

"Excuse me," said the lady. She was older than Mum—almost as old as the woman who had spoken to me on the subway—and I thought she looked like she might be Indian. Her thick silvery hair was cut short, and she was wearing a long blue dress that floated around her legs.

Kat turned and squinted up at her. "Hello?" she said.

"Hello," said the lady. "How old are you?"

"Er," said Kat, wiping the juice off her chin. "Sixteen. Why?"

This was another of Kat's lies. She is fourteen, and not even fourteen and a half: her birthday is on March 15.

"I love your shirt," said the lady. "Where did you get it?"

Kat sat bolt upright. "I," she said, "I . . . I . . ." Kat's brain was suffering from a mini Ice Age. "I made it." And even though she had been Mean Kat about the Magnum crust, I decided that I would help her.

"She designs clothes," I told the lady. "She's trying to be discovered. Are you here to discover her?"

The lady laughed, even though I had not said anything that was funny.

"I'm here to see the *Hidden in Plain Sight* exhibition," she said. "It's new. But I seem to have found you as well. Funny how plans change. If you made that, then you have a real flair for clothing design. Are you hoping to study it?"

"Yes, but Mum and Dad don't think I should," said Kat.

"But of course you should!" said the lady. "Here—I'll give you my card. You have your parents call me and I'll tell them what's what." She clicked open her silky purse and pulled out a white square with black words printed on it. She put this into Kat's hand—Kat was still having trouble with her brain Ice Age—and nodded down at us all. "Now I must go. I'll be late for my exhibition window. Good day!"

And she went walking up the steps into the Metropolitan Museum of Art, her blue skirt blowing around her.

"Oh," said Kat. "Oh. Oh. *Oh! Look!*"

I looked. It was still the same white square I had seen before.

"Jas Singh," said Kat, her voice coming out of her mouth in a gasp. "House of Cyriax. *Oh.* She's very, very— she's very, very, very . . ." And without explaining what Jas Singh was, she burst into tears. "This is amazing. Out of the blue, like that!"

This made sense, because the woman had been wearing a blue skirt. What didn't make sense was that Kat was crying. Nothing bad had happened.

"That's the first positive thing we've heard all day,"

said Salim, and he took a melted bite of his Good Humor bar. "All we've been hearing is what *didn't* happen. The painting didn't go out through the roof. It didn't stay in the museum, or if it did, we don't know where it is. No one saw it go out of the front or the back door, but one of those *must* be right. How are we supposed to know which one is true?"

"Ted?" said Kat, and she nudged me. "Now would be the time for you to have a brain wave."

I squeezed my eyes shut, so that the New York August afternoon blinked out and left me with just blue-and-red swirls in front of my eyes. Sometimes I like to pretend that the only part of the world that exists is the part that I can see. So I pretended that the whole world was swirls. Then I imagined that the swirls were my brain waves, and I could see them refracting back from the inside of my eyelids. *Refraction* is how white light becomes a rainbow. There is a rainbow in *In the Black Square,* and so it is a painting about light, even though Kandinsky had used no real light, only paint. If he had wanted to make a painting with actual light, he would have had to use a camera, the way Salim does.

That was an interesting thought. I opened my eyes.

All of New York rushed in—the yellow taxis and the gray street and the blue sky and the white steps, with shadows from the sun.

"What do you think?" asked Kat.

"Hrumm," I said. "I need to look at Salim's camera."

Salim pulled his camera round on his neck so we could see its little display window. Last time I had been with Salim, he'd had a camera with film in it. Now he had a digital camera. Everything had changed.

He began to click through the photographs he had taken over the last two days. I saw the case all over again through Salim's eyes. His pictures made a record of what we had done, and who we had seen—but they were unique to Salim. If I had taken them, they would have been different. I liked that. Salim was an artist too.

There was the picture of Billy on the pavement, Sarah in her office, Ty with his tools, Jacob outside the German bar, Helen and Lana with their tools in the garden, Sandra's fridge, with Kat looking inside it, the empty Guggenheim with its lights off, Lionel in the gift shop next to the posters. . . .

"Stop," I said. "Go back to Helen and Lana."

Salim flicked backward. There was the picture of

Helen and Lana again, in front of the fountain, their tools piled up on the ground. Hammers, wrenches, nails and washers and screws.

"Look," I said. "Look!"

"At what?" said Kat. Her voice was sharp and loud. She didn't see what I saw.

"The tools," I said.

Then Salim understood. "Ted!" he said. "You're right! They don't need all those tools to mend a paving stone. It's like all the extra things we found behind that wall. There were so many of them—not just washers and screws, but actual *tools*. What if they are taking extra tools and materials out of the museums they work at, to sell?"

"Do tools cost lots of money?" asked Kat.

"Yes!" said Salim. "Ty told me once. They're so expensive. You have to get them ordered specially. What if Helen has been ordering extra, with the museums paying for them, and then selling them?"

"That would be why Helen stayed in the museum for such a long time when the alarm went off!" said Kat. "She was packing up the extra tools and hiding them so the police didn't ask about them. And that's why Lana lied for her, because she must be part of it. It's just like

Lionel and the food! But hold on—if *that's* what they were doing, then who stole the painting? Does that mean it was Hank and Ben? But—how did they get it out? Was it in Hank's uniform? Are we missing something?"

I thought about Lana, and Helen, and working together, and something finally clicked into place in my head.

"No, we aren't," I said. "We haven't missed anything. We know everything we need to solve the case."

49

BRAIN WAVES AND LIGHTBULBS

We had thought that there were pieces of the puzzle that we still had not found. We had assumed that someone had seen something that we did not know about, or that the thief had to have smuggled the painting out of the museum in a way that we could not imagine.

But what if that was the wrong way of looking at the problem?

What if we *did* know everything we needed to? What if we *had* seen everything?

Sherlock Holmes, who was a great detective, even if he was made up, said in one of the stories about him, "Once you eliminate the impossible, whatever remains, no matter how improbable, must be the truth." It was impossible for the painting to have been taken out through the skylight, because Gabriel hadn't been there to collect it, and no one else had been seen climbing on the scaffolding. It was impossible for the painting to have been taken out through the back door, because Billy hadn't seen it happen. It was impossible for the painting to have been taken out through the front door, because *we* hadn't seen it happen, and later, when the police were there, they hadn't seen it either. So the only theory that was left . . .

"The painting is still inside the Guggenheim," I said.

"Don't be stupid, Ted!" said Kat.

"I'm not being stupid!" I said. "I'm eliminating impossible things. The thief could not have taken the painting out of the museum without someone seeing it, so it is almost certainly still inside. We just have to work out where it is, and how the thief is planning to take it out."

I closed my eyes again, put my hands over my ears and breathed deeply. I had to think. I twisted the Guggenheim, its ramp, its triangular staircases and its long banks of lights, around in my head, circles within circles, just the way Frank Lloyd Wright had wanted. But the Guggenheim was not exactly the way Frank Lloyd Wright had imagined it. Things change, the way exhibitions at museums change, and people change and have ambitions.

I thought about voices, and telephone lines, and text messages. I thought about hiding paintings, and smoke bombs, and tools. I thought about the lights in Times Square, their patterns in the sky, and all the hands I had imagined. I thought that when people say *the Guggenheim*, they mean the big central space with the ramp, but it is really more complicated than that. It has stairs and tower galleries and gift shops and offices.

Then I thought about all the things we had seen on our quest around New York. I thought about Effortless Light Moving. I thought about photographs and paintings, what was worthless and what was priceless, and how different those two things had turned out to be. I thought about figures of speech, and people using language precisely but also saying things they did not exactly mean. I thought about all the people I had met who were similar to me, even though I had been worried that they would be different. I thought about families, and friends, and people working together. I thought about outsides, and insides, and all the surprising things we had discovered about people: Ty and his ambition to become an architect, Lionel and his children, Jacob and his oompah music, Sandra's gluten allergy and the Pop-Tarts in her fridge. I thought about Detective Leigh and how he moved his arms and legs stiffly, like I do. There was one other person who had moved stiffly, I thought—but at first I could not remember who. Then I thought of green leaves and blue sky, and I knew where the memory came from. Dad has taught me that another way of saying brain wave is *lightbulb moment*. I imagined a lightbulb switching on, and I knew the one other person we had met in New York who would enjoy a visual pun like that.

And I knew the answer to the Guggenheim Mystery.

50

THE GUGGENHEIM SOLUTION

"I know who took the painting," I told Kat and Salim. "I know why, and I know how, and I know how they are going to try to get it out of the Guggenheim."

"You don't!" gasped Kat.

"I do!" I said. Although I am learning how to lie, I wouldn't lie about something important like this.

"OH MY LORD!" shrieked Kat. Her arms shot up into the air and the sparkles on her shirt glittered.

"You're not making it up?" asked Salim. His face was still not sure. "You really know? How?"

"Because of Pop-Tarts and ice cream and building plans," I said. "Because of ladders, and all the hands in

Times Square. Because of the way *The Scream* is not a painting of a scream—it's a painting of someone *hearing* a scream. It's the other way round from how you think it is at first, and that's exactly what happened with this theft. We thought the painting was outside, when it was really inside. We thought that it had already been stolen, but it hasn't actually been stolen yet. We have to hurry! We have to go back to the Guggenheim and *prove* that the thief is not Aunt Gloria."

"What? Of course it's been stolen!" said Salim.

"Come on, Salim. Let Ted show us!" shouted Kat.

And then all three of us were running back up Fifth Avenue, back toward the Guggenheim.

The skin on my arms and neck itched. My lungs felt small. My shoes hit the pavement, and the heat from it spread up through the plastic underneath them and the cotton of my socks into the soles of my feet and made them sweat. But I made myself concentrate. I had to be a hero like Odysseus, for Salim, and Aunt Gloria, and Kat, and also myself, because I could be a person who came to a new place and learned its pattern. I could change my plans, and still be Ted Spark.

I saw the blue-and-white banners, and the silver-and-blue scaffolding that was now the Guggenheim's exoskeleton. The white outside it had become an inside, and the first time I saw it, I should have realized that even something that seems so clean and smooth has layers. The Guggenheim has been added to since 1959. It has a gift shop and a tower. It has been repainted and rewired and reorganized, and the thief knew that, and had used it to hide the painting in plain sight. They had taken Frank Lloyd Wright's circles and triangles and used them to commit a crime.

I went straight in through the revolving front door of the museum, past the shiny round metal plaque on the floor that said LET EACH MAN EXERCISE THE ART HE KNOWS. That also made me sad, because I knew that the thief had done exactly that. They had used what they knew to trick us all, and frame Aunt Gloria.

Inside, the maintenance crew was working again, the noise from their voices and their tools bouncing off the white walls. Helen and Lana were at work on another false wall, their tool bag between them. Jacob was polishing the floor. Ben was drilling holes for paintings. I couldn't see Ty.

Lionel saw us. "Hey!" he said. "What are you doing back already?"

"Salim left his wallet in the gift shop," I said. This was my eighth lie.

Salim and Kat looked at me. I saw the corners of Kat's mouth twitch. "Yeah," said Salim. "My mistake. Can we just . . ."

Lionel waved us past, and we went into the gift shop.

Ty was there, standing on a stepladder, fixing a lightbulb. His long bag of tools was next to his feet. "Hey!" he said to us, looking round. "What are you doing here?"

"Um," said Salim. "We're . . ."

I looked at Kat. For once, I needed our brain waves to be operating on the same frequency. I saw her eyes widen, and her mouth open.

"We're looking for a present for Auntie Glo," she said. "Ted, which print did you want?"

I walked toward the drawers of posters. My knees *felt like water,* which is a figure of speech but at that moment did not feel very figurative at all.

"What are you doing?" said a voice behind me. Sandra was standing in the gift-shop doorway, her mouth straight and flat and her eyebrows raised. Lionel was just behind her. I decided to ignore her. "Ted!" she said. "Ted Spark! What are you doing?"

I reached forward and pulled open a drawer, taking out the poster tube on the top of the pile, the one that had been empty this morning.

It was not empty any longer. I popped open the end of the tube and out slid a heavy roll of material that scratched my hands. It fell onto the floor and opened, and there were the curves and colors of *In the Black Square*. It was true, I noticed, that you could see the brushstrokes Kandinsky had used. It really did not look like the prints of itself at all.

"We have found the missing painting," I said. "Sandra and Ty were about to steal it."

51

SILENCE AND NOISE

I am beginning to realize that silences sound different in different circumstances. Sometimes they can be soft. Sometimes they can be full of the last noise that happened, its waves still bouncing further and further out into the universe.

When you have just accused two people of stealing a painting worth $20 million, the silence is very full indeed. It was full of people breathing. No one said anything for 9.7 seconds (I counted by looking at my weather watch), which is long enough for the fastest man in the world to run one hundred meters.

"This is utterly ridiculous!" said Sandra, 9.8 seconds later.

"No way," said Salim. "No *way!*"

Lionel, still standing behind her, used a bad swear word, and then began to speak very quickly into his walkie-talkie.

Ty had turned toward us on his ladder. He stared at the painting but didn't say anything. His mouth was closed, and his face was blank. He didn't move.

"But . . . how did it get here?" asked Lionel. "I saw you guys half an hour ago—it wasn't here then!"

"Because it was only just moved here," I explained. "Sandra cut it from its frame in the gallery, then Ty hid it in the broken light fixtures on the second level of the ramp, where he had been just before the smoke bombs went off. He said he was up on a ladder, which is how I knew that for certain. The lights aren't working at the moment, so the painting wouldn't show up as a dark strip. The fixtures are over a meter long and triangular, which means that a rolled-up painting could fit in there. In fact, it's one of the only places in this museum that a painting that size could be hidden—and Ty was the only person working in the right place, at the right time, to hide it.

"After he had hidden the painting, Ty smashed the frame into pieces that would fit into his baggy work trousers and walked out of the Guggenheim. Later he hid the pieces in a bush in Central Park. After that he and Sandra waited until the police had left the museum and let the maintenance crew back in to finish working on the new exhibition. Then Ty got the painting out from the lights, took it down to the gift shop and put it into the empty tube that Sandra had left there earlier. Later today Sandra was going to come into the gift shop and buy a new print for her collection—which was really the painting."

"Ted, don't be silly. Why would I steal the painting?" asked Sandra. Her lip was wobbling, and her arms were folded.

"Because you've worked at the Guggenheim for five years," I said. "You know all about how it's designed, so you know that the lights would be a good hiding place. But you don't make as much money as Aunt Gloria because you're only an assistant curator. You don't have much money, but you like nice things that are expensive. Like Manolo Blahnik shoes. You also don't like Kandinsky, so if you had to cut a painting out of its frame to steal it, you wouldn't mind as much if it was a Kandinsky painting. You also work in the same office as Aunt Gloria. You had the best opportunity to steal her credit card on Monday. You're a woman. Sarah at Effortless Light Moving said that it was a woman who called, and Ty's voice is too deep to pretend to be Aunt Gloria. And you've got a big handbag."

I remembered Sandra telling us that she didn't like Kandinsky. I had thought that meant she wouldn't steal a painting by him, but instead it meant the opposite: that she wouldn't *mind* stealing a Kandinsky to get the money from it. It was just another way of looking at the same thing.

"So what's my handbag have to do with it?" asked Sandra. I could see that her body was worried, and I knew that her voice was lying.

"You could have hidden smoke bombs in it," I said. "We saw you come into the gallery just before the smoke alarms went off. You could have come up the side stairs and dropped the bombs on the way. I realized that the person who set off the smoke bombs must have hidden them somewhere—they could not have just held them in their hands. And you could have put a knife in your handbag too, to cut the painting out of its frame. Lionel would trust you—he wouldn't have looked in your bag.

"After the smoke alarms went off, you ran down the ramp with us, but then you left us at the main door. You could have run back up the ramp into the gallery and cut the painting out of its frame then. But you couldn't have smashed the frame in those high-heeled shoes you were wearing, and you couldn't have made sure the camera systems were off before. You needed someone strong and good with electrical things, someone who has a clever brain to plan tricks. Someone like Ty.

"You met Ty in the gallery, gave him the painting, and he ran back up the ramp, climbed up his ladder and pushed the painting into the light fixtures he had been working on. Then he went out of the front door with everyone else. Apart from us, he was the fifth person to come out, which is strange, because he wasn't that high up the ramp. He only just came out in front of Jacob. But it makes more sense if he was moving slowly because he had something in the legs of his trousers that made him walk stiffly.

"When we saw him in Central Park, he was moving oddly. I didn't know why, but it makes sense now, if he had just got rid of the bits of frame in the bushes!" I took a deep breath.

"What did you mean about the Pop-Tarts?" whispered Kat to me.

"Sandra can't eat Pop-Tarts," I said. "She's gluten-intolerant. So that made me realize that she had had someone in her apartment who was not allergic to gluten, and probably someone young too. Someone who would like to eat Pop-Tarts. I realized that Sandra would have needed help from someone on the crew, and Ty is the youngest. We thought that no one on the crew liked Sandra—and we thought that if there were two thieves working together, they had to like each other, or be family. But we weren't thinking in the right way. It didn't matter whether Sandra liked the person who helped her steal the painting. She *made* them help her, because that is the kind of person she is.

"Ty also fitted with the way the crime was planned. He is the kind of person who would think of smoke bombs, because he likes jokes and pranks, like Salim. He also likes puns, and wordplay. Remember how he used the word *cracked* in two different ways, and referred back to it later? He told us that he *didn't see nothing,* which was literally true. That was also wordplay. And Effortless

Light Moving was his joke too. He sent the police after a van with a lightbulb on it, when all the time the painting was hidden next to a real lightbulb."

"Is this true?" Lionel asked Ty.

"No," said Ty. He was still very stiff and I saw that his hands were shaking.

That was when Lieutenant Leigh walked into the gift shop.

52

IN THE NICK OF TIME

His lips were turned down, but when his eyes behind their glasses saw *In the Black Square* lying on the floor, they got very wide.

"Where . . . ?" he said. "How . . . ?"

"Sandra and Ty stole it," I told him. "We found it *just in the nick of time.* The frame is in a bush in Central Park, broken up. The painting used to be in the light fixtures on the second floor, but it was just moved to the gift shop. Sandra was going to buy it as soon as the museum shop opened again."

"I think the kid's onto something," said Lionel, nodding. "You've got to listen to him."

*　*　*

After that, things moved at New York speed. Lionel put his hands on Sandra's and Ty's shoulders (he didn't look happy about this, and neither did they) while Lieutenant Leigh took out his phone and spoke quickly into it. Seven minutes later, two blue-and-white cars with New York plates pulled up outside the gift shop, and three police officers scrambled out and put Ty and Sandra in handcuffs. I thought this was exciting, because I had never actually seen people put in handcuffs before. But then I looked at Salim's face and saw that its skin was tight, its eyes looking down and its mouth straight.

"Why did it have to be Ty?" he said. "I thought he was helping us. He kept texting to see how we were getting on!"

"He was texting because he wanted to know how close we were to finding the painting," I said. "He was helping Sandra because he needed the money to become an architect."

This explanation made sense to me, but it didn't seem to please Salim. And I understood. It was true, but it was also sad.

As Ty was being taken out of the gift-shop door, he

295

turned back to where we were standing. "Salim!" he said. "Man. Hey, I'm sorry."

"You framed my mum," said Salim. "You helped steal the painting, and you would have let her go to jail for you!"

"Yeah, but . . . ," said Ty. "It's just a painting. No one got hurt."

"*I* got hurt," said Salim, and he folded his arms and stared at a spot on the ceiling.

Kat stood next to him and folded her arms, and I copied them. I thought I was getting very good at this. We stood there, and Ty and Sandra were put into the cars and driven away. It felt like some of the air was draining out of the universe.

Lieutenant Leigh took out a pair of white latex gloves from his pocket and went over to where the painting was. He bent over it, and I could tell that his body knew exactly how to deal with it. It wasn't awkward and stiff now. He rolled up the painting in a gentle, perfect curve, and then slid it very carefully back into the tube it had come from. Once he had done that, he breathed out slowly, and his lips went up. He turned his head to face us.

"You're very lucky kids," he said.

"It was not luck!" I said. "We deduced the truth by

ruling out impossible things one by one. We worked together. The painting had to be in the museum. There was
only one place a long, rolled-up painting could be hidden,
and only one person who could have hidden it there—Ty.
But he couldn't have done it on his own."

"Well, then," said Lieutenant Leigh. "You're very
smart. And I'm very lucky. I came here today because
all our other leads had gone cold. The crate we spent
almost two days chasing was found in a warehouse this
morning, empty. The surveillance cameras in the area
around the museum had come up with nothing. The
smoke bombs and moving companies had been bought
with Gloria McCloud's credit card, but she wasn't admit-
ting it under questioning."

"That's because she didn't do it! Sandra and Ty did.
She's innocent!" said Salim.

"I didn't believe her before, but that's certainly how
it seems now," said Lieutenant Leigh. "But we have to
make sure." Then his walkie-talkie buzzed. He listened
to it, and his eyebrows rose above the rims of his glasses
again. "We've found the smashed-up pieces of frame," he
said to me and Kat and Salim. "They were exactly where
you told us they would be: in a bush in Central Park, near
the ice cream stand. Well, well!"

"Well, well," I said.

"He means *good work*, Ted!" Kat whispered to me.

I noticed that Lionel wasn't speaking to the detective, or helping us explain the case. Instead, he was wiping his face again, left to right and then right to left and then left to right, but I saw four beads of sweat on his right temple that he had missed. From this I deduced that Lionel was hot, but he was also nervous. I thought, and understood why this was: because he had also committed a crime, a very small one. He was worried that Lieutenant Leigh would want to punish him as well. Lionel had done a bad thing, but he had done it for a good reason. It was a little like what Ty had done—but only a little.

I wanted to help Lionel. "You won't be searching the museum anymore, will you?" I asked Lieutenant Leigh.

"What?" asked Lieutenant Leigh. He wasn't paying attention to me. "No."

"That is good," I said. "Also, Lionel is an excellent security guard. He helped us solve the case, and he is very kind. You should tell the director that he has done a good job." It felt like lying, not telling Lieutenant Leigh about what Lionel had done—but I was realizing that lying can sometimes be a good thing.

The detective's lips turned up. "Sure," he said, looking at Lionel at last. "I guess he has."

I was pleased.

"Now," said Lieutenant Leigh. "I think the three of you need to come down to the station and answer some more questions. I'm not gonna arrest you, I promise—I just want to understand what happened."

And so, three minutes and fifty seconds later, Salim, Kat and I were all sitting in the back of another blue-and-white police car, on the way to the police station ourselves.

53

AT THE STATION

When we got to the police station, which was a tall red building with yellow-and-blue arches and writing on the glass above the front door that said 19TH PRECINCT, there was a lot of shouting.

This is because three minutes after we walked through the door and were sent into a small room with a square white table and six hard white chairs, like school chairs, Aunt Gloria and Mum came in.

Aunt Gloria's makeup had run down her face, and Mum's hair was sticking up on one side of her head as though she had been sleeping against the wall. When they saw us, Aunt Gloria burst into tears and ran at Salim and hugged him, then shouted at him, then hugged him again. Mum hugged Kat, and hugged me, even though I tried to step away from her.

"We solved the mystery, Mum!" I said. "We've saved you, Aunt Gloria!"

"WHAT?" cried Aunt Gloria.

"WHAT?" cried Mum.

They were being very loud. I felt my head go to one side.

"LISTEN!" shouted Kat. "*Mum! Aunt Gloria!* It's true! We did it. I mean, Ted worked it out in the end, but I *did* help, and so did Salim. We found the painting! *And* we worked out who stole it, so the police know it wasn't you, Auntie Glo. They're going to let you out soon!"

Salim grinned, crossed his arms and said, "What Kat said."

Aunt Gloria gaped, and so did Mum. We had to tell them the whole story, which bothered me because it took a very long time. But saying everything again made me see some points in the pattern that I had missed.

"I just can't believe Sandra would do such a thing!" Aunt Gloria kept repeating, very loudly. "She was my rock! She was always there for me! She knew everything!"

I translated what Aunt Gloria had said, looking at it

upside down, just the way I had with Sandra and the Kandinsky. Sandra had been at the Guggenheim for years before Aunt Gloria arrived. This meant that even though she acted nicely to Aunt Gloria and Salim, she might also be annoyed that Aunt Gloria was more important than her. Sandra knew everything, including where to cut the cameras to put them out of action, and where you could set off smoke bombs without anyone else noticing. She set one off in the stairwell, and another on the second-floor ramp, so it had rolled down to where the fire crew had found it later.

"That Ty boy, though," Aunt Gloria went on. "Salim, you should never have spent time with him."

"Mum!" said Salim. "That's not fair! He was always nice to me. He didn't exactly tell me that he was going to steal a painting, did he? If you didn't know about Sandra, then I shouldn't have to have known about Ty. I liked him, all right? And *you* liked *Sandra*."

"Well . . . ," said Aunt Gloria. "Well—oh, Salim, I knew this city was a bad idea!"

"No way! I love it here. I helped solve the crime, didn't I?" said Salim. "Mum, I don't need to be protected anymore. And we can't leave, and go back to Manchester. We're different now."

Mum smiled. She murmured that Aunt Gloria had almost been sent to prison, which would have made her *extremely* different. It was the sort of joke that Dad would usually make, which let me know that Mum was missing him.

Kat said, "You have to listen to me too, Mum," and she held out the card the woman on the steps of the Met had given her. She told Mum that the woman had said she had potential, and that had made Kat sure that she was right to want to do art and design GCSEs. Mum stopped smiling.

"Kat, you're too young!" she said. "I've told you, no one knows what they want to be when they are fourteen."

Kat stuck out her chin and said, "I'm not too young. I'm growing up all the time. And I *do* know what I want to be. I bet *you* did too, Mum."

"Oh, your mum nursed anything she could get her hands on," said Aunt Gloria. "I remember her making me pretend I had a broken leg when I was three and she was six. She gave me a spoonful of something from a bottle to make me better, only it ended up being your granddad's gin, and I was sick all over the sofa."

"GLO!" shouted Mum. "You are not helping! Oh, Kat, can't we talk about this another time?"

"We can," said Kat. "*If* you promise to actually think about it and not just tell me off, and *if* you promise that I can do art and design as well as biology."

Mum rested her cupped hands against her head. "Kat, you have got me while I am weak," she said. "But . . . all right."

Kat whooped, and Salim high-fived her.

That was when Lieutenant Leigh came back in to see us.

54

CRACKED CASE

He told us that Sandra had confessed. Words *poured out of her,* said Lieutenant Leigh, and I imagined a river splashing from Sandra's throat, each word a water molecule.

She had told him that she needed the money, and she had heard of someone who would buy *In the Black Square* from her. She knew she could cut it out of its frame cleanly (I wondered if she had practiced on some prints in her apartment), and where it could be hidden, but she needed someone to help her with the more physical part. She decided that Ty would be the one, because he could cut the wiring in the lights and the camera systems, and he could get into the light fixtures easily. She told him that she would have him fired if he didn't help, so it was her idea—but Ty had become very interested in planning, and most of what happened in the end was his idea.

They worked everything out in Sandra's apartment (which was the reason for the Pop-Tarts—just as I had thought, Sandra had bought them for Ty). They had been waiting for an exhibition changeover, when the museum would be empty and the director would be away.

Sandra decided to frame Aunt Gloria from the beginning, but when Aunt Gloria told everyone that her English relatives were coming to stay this week, and she would only come to the museum on Thursday morning to show us around, they realized that the theft had to happen on Thursday.

Once Sandra had set off the smoke bombs, and we had gone out of the museum, Sandra had run back up the ramp (through the smoke) into the second-floor tower gallery. The cameras in the gallery weren't working, so Sandra couldn't be seen. There was also not as much smoke there as there was in the rotunda. She took a knife out of her handbag and cut the painting out of its frame. She rolled it up and then carried it, along with the frame, out to the entrance of the gallery, where Ty was waiting. He broke the frame into pieces with his boot—the noise of the alarm covered up any noise he made—then ran back up the ramp to put the painting into the light fixture, before going slowly back down the ramp, with the pieces of the frame in his trousers. The whole thing took less than three minutes, and then they were out of the building with everyone else.

The plan was to trick the police into thinking that the painting had been taken out of the Guggenheim by the moving van. They would follow it, and then the next van, as they went all around New York, and by the time they found the crate and realized that it was empty, Ty would have had the chance to get back into the Guggenheim, take the painting out of the light fixture and leave it in the gift shop, in the empty poster tube, for Sandra to collect and buy.

"Very clever," the lieutenant said, nodding his head. "They would have outwitted us. Good work, Ted, Salim and Kat."

His lips turned up at me. I tried to make my mouth mirror his, the way I did with Salim.

"If you're ever looking for a job, you should think of us," said the lieutenant, and then he closed one eye in a wink behind his glasses. Usually this is the sign that someone is joking, but the rest of the lieutenant's face was serious. So I decided that he was telling the truth. I felt pleased. He held out his hand and dropped a white card on the table—the same sort of card that Jas Singh had given Kat. I reached out my hand and picked it up. It read LT. DONOVAN LEIGH, and there was a telephone number after his name.

I looked up from the card to Lieutenant Leigh.

"Thank you," I said.

It felt good to think that I had made a friend in New York, and I had seven friends after all.

"I have to say, I feel terrible for that boy Ty, even if he did end up helping Sandra," said Mum when Lieutenant Leigh had gone. "He's so young. Glo, this is dreadful."

I also felt very mixed up when I thought about Ty: sad and angry and confused. Ty had tricked us all, pretending to be our friend when he was really not. He had needed money to help him get what he wanted, which was to become an architect. But committing a crime is a choice, just like everything anyone does. Some things do not seem like choices, like the moment I got on the wrong subway train, but I still could have gone the other way, and if I had, things would be different. We all feel as though we are being pulled in different directions by patterns that we cannot even see, but actually we are making our own patterns, every single second. We can choose to be heroes or villains.

Then Salim said, "I want to see him. I want to see Ty."

We were shown into another small white room with a white table and six white chairs. This time only one person was sitting on one of them. It was Ty. His arms were leaning on the table and his head was leaning on his arms, and I knew that the emotion he was feeling was sadness.

"Ty," said Salim, and Ty looked up at us. His eyes were red, and his mouth was turned down.

"Salim, man," he said. "I'm sorry. I didn't mean what I said before. I'm really, really sorry."

"So am I," said Salim.

"We're still friends," said Ty. "Right? I just . . . made a mistake. It started out as Sandra's idea. She told me if I helped her, I'd be rich. I could have everything I wanted, and we'd never be caught, because most art thieves aren't caught, and anyway it was just a *painting*. It didn't matter."

"Of course it mattered," said Salim.

"I know that now," said Ty, and his head dropped

down onto his arms again. "But then I just got, I don't know, interested in the planning. It was just another problem to solve, something else to build, and then we were doing it and it felt like a joke. The cameras even went down on their own on Tuesday—I barely had to do anything. But after we'd done it, it didn't feel like a joke anymore. I was so worried that you'd work it out. And I thought that they'd just let your mom off. But then the lieutenant really thought she'd done it when he arrested her. He wasn't going to let her go."

I thought that even though Ty had been one of the thieves, and he had helped plan the crime, he was right that it was very hard to say no to Sandra. I remembered the way she had told us what to do when we stayed with her. Then I knew for certain that Ty was still a clever, good person, even though he had done a bad thing.

I had thought that a missing painting would be a simple mystery to solve, with no emotions in it, but it had turned out to be very difficult to understand.

55

A CHANGE IS AS GOOD AS . . .

It was very strange trying to have a holiday in New York after we had solved a mystery. Aunt Gloria and Mum became extra cheerful, saying lots of loud things about how *exciting* New York was, and how there was *so much to do*.

The next day, instead of resting, we were dragged onto the subway, and then off again, and up tall buildings and down again. We went to a toy shop with a man outside it pretending to be a Buckingham Palace guard, and a clock on the wall inside with a face and eyes that moved. Noise shrilled into my ears from ten different directions and lights flashed. We went to Central Park, and its zoo, and saw the lonely polar bear swimming round and round his enclosure. It was all exactly like my guidebook.

But something had changed in me since our first day in New York. I realized as we stood at the top of the Empire State Building that evening, with New York shining in all directions like a lit map, and a wind coming in from the sea against my face, that all the noise and light didn't make me feel as though I was about to disintegrate into approximately a billion pieces. My hand flapped, but that was only for reassurance. I had traveled all over New York, and that quest had changed me.

Salim had his camera up to his eye and was taking pictures. I thought he was taking pictures of the city, until I followed the path of his lens and saw Kat, with her arms up, her face pushing into the wind. She didn't look beautiful, or like a model. She looked like my sister.

"Good picture," said Salim to me, lowering the camera. This was the first thing he had said for quite a while.

"Can I have a copy?" I asked.

"You can have as many as you want," said Salim. I imagined thousands of copies of the picture of Kat, flying off the edge of the Empire State Building's deck and whirling through the air. I liked that thought. Although some art is important because there is only one of it, I think photographs are always just as good, because each print is the photograph itself.

I didn't know how to say what I really meant, so I said, "Thank you, Salim," and went to stand next to Mum.

"My Ted," said Mum, and she put her arm round me. I took a deep breath, and didn't let my body flinch. "You're something special, you know that?"

"Yes, Mum," I said, because I did.

There was a message from Lieutenant Leigh for Aunt Gloria on the answering machine when we got home. He had good news. The police were charging Sandra as the main thief of *In the Black Square*. Ty was going to be charged with helping her steal it, and hiding it, but because he only helped, he wouldn't go to prison for as long, even if he was found guilty.

I felt good about this. I didn't like thinking about Ty in prison. I hoped that he would be able to study to become an architect while he was there, or when he got out.

Mum called Dad in London, and they had a long talk while Kat paced in circles around Aunt Gloria's white sofa and chewed her nails. But in the end she didn't need to worry, because Mum came back out of Aunt Gloria's room with a smile on her face. The smile meant that Kat was allowed to take art and design GCSEs, and also to apply for fashion design internship programs in London next summer, including at the House of Cyriax.

"My clever niece!" said Aunt Gloria. "Art does run in our family!"

Kat squealed, and hugged Mum and Aunt Gloria and Salim, and then she went dancing around the sofa, arms waving. She was Hurricane Kat again, but she was whirling with happiness, not anger.

I woke up at 3:32 a.m. New York time, on the day we were going to fly home to London and Dad, and heard Salim and Kat whispering again. They were both sitting on Salim's futon, and their heads were bent close together.

"I'm glad Aunt Faith listened to you," said Salim.

"Me too," said Kat. "And I'm glad Auntie Glo listened to you." Then she sighed. "I wish you weren't so far away, though," she said. "I'm going to miss you this year."

I agreed with Kat. Although I was happy that Salim didn't have to go back to Manchester because Aunt Gloria was in prison, I realized that there would be a gap in the pattern of our family without them. New York was very far away from London.

"Hey!" said Salim. "I'll email you! Or we can Skype."

"I suppose," said Kat, and she sighed again.

"Listen!" said Salim. "We're a team. You, me and Ted. We don't have to be on the same continent for that. Right, Ted?"

"Hrumm," I said, because I hadn't realized that Salim knew I was awake.

Then Kat laughed, and Salim laughed too. It was good to know that they really *were* my friends, as well as my family.

Our plane took off that afternoon. Kat's head was bobbing along to the music on her iPod, and Mum was bent over her magazine, and I stared down at the clouds below me. They were altocumulus, which meant that change was on the way, and I thought this was good. I had been to New York, and learned its patterns and weather systems, and gone on a quest like Odysseus and become a hero and solved a mystery, and even though I had felt myself change, I also knew that I was still the same Ted I had always been. My brain was still unique, and it was still good. It had helped me solve two mysteries that no one else could, and I thought that if I ever found any more mysteries in my life, I would know what to do.

I sat back in my seat, and felt the plane jump and judder through my body. I was Ted Spark. And I was happy with that.

AUTHOR'S NOTE

It is strange to come to the end of a book and acknowledge that you wish you had not written it. Of course, that is not literally true: I am proud of *The Guggenheim Mystery* and loved every moment of creating Ted's New York mystery.

But all the same, it is a tragedy that I ever sat down to write it. Siobhan Dowd created Ted Spark and his family in *The London Eye Mystery*. She was contracted to write it and one other book, simply referred to as *The Guggenheim Mystery*, but only a few months after *The London Eye Mystery* was published, in August 2007, she died from cancer at the age of forty-seven. She never got to even begin planning *her* Guggenheim Mystery, and so the Siobhan

Dowd Trust had to look for another author to write it in her stead. They approached me in 2015, to see if I would be interested, and I knew that I absolutely would. I began the project with only Siobhan's characters and those three words to go on, and the story built from there.

I loved *The London Eye Mystery* from the first time I read it. Siobhan was an incredible writer, and all her books are marvelous, but *The London Eye Mystery* feels particularly special to me. It is, quite simply, one of the best-constructed mysteries I have ever come across, and so the thought of carrying on Ted's story was both extremely exciting and completely daunting. All I can say is that I have done my best, and I am grateful for all the pointers I have been given from all the people who loved her. When you talk to anyone who worked with Siobhan and her books, their faces light up. She means so much to everyone she knew, and everyone has a personal story of her kindness to tell.

Before I was given *The Guggenheim Mystery* as a project, I did not know much about the Guggenheim itself—apart from the fact that it was a museum, in New York, that showed modern art. But as soon as I began to read about it, I realized why Siobhan had chosen it as the setting of Ted's second adventure. If Ted is a different sort of detective, the Guggenheim, with its curving ramp, its rotunda shape and its insistence on viewing art from all angles at once, is a different sort of museum. Ted would be perfectly at home there—and if anything were to happen to one of the paintings, he would be the perfect person to solve the mystery.

Once I knew that I was going to write my first art heist, I had to think carefully about which painting I wanted to steal. I ended up choosing *In the Black Square* by Vasily Kandinsky. In case you were wondering, this painting, and its artist, are absolutely real, and you may google them both. Kandinsky (1866–1944) was a Russian abstract artist who worked with colors and shapes. His paintings are bright and exciting, and I love looking at them. I thought that Ted would enjoy the weather in *In the Black Square*—it would stretch him in exactly the right way, and make him think about art, and why we value it so much.

I have tried to be as truthful and as close to reality as I could with the setting itself, and worked with the Guggenheim to get my facts straight, but at the end of the day, *I made this book up*. There are some places (precise details of the exhibition I used, for example) where I've had to take certain liberties with the truth. Forgive me!

One more note on museums. Like Salim, I grew up with a mother who worked in one. Mine was the director of education at the Ashmolean Museum in Oxford, and so I spent many hours wandering around the museum as a child. In fact, my mother was part of the Ashmolean staff in 2000, when one of its most famous art thefts occurred. I promise you, though, that she didn't do it any more than Aunt Gloria did. Thieves broke into the museum on New Year's Eve, using the noise of the fireworks to mask their entry. To make sure that the cameras did not catch them, they set off smoke bombs in the gallery, and escaped with a Cézanne worth £3 million. So if you've been wondering why I chose the method I did for my own made-up art theft . . . now you know.

ACKNOWLEDGMENTS

Thank you to my perceptive, thoughtful and direct early readers: Kathie Booth Stevens, Charlie Morris, Anne Miller, Mariam Khan, Wei Ming Kam, Holly Campbell from the Guggenheim (huge thanks to JiaJia Fei, who put us in touch), Simon Houlton and Leonie Bennett, and Michele Butler and Jordan Lynton (who were introduced to me by Aimée Felone). Your feedback helped shape this book, and I am enormously grateful to you.

Huge thanks to Donal Emerson and Oona Emerson, and to the Siobhan Dowd Trust, for supporting this book and giving me insight into Ted's interests and ambitions. Thanks to Hilary Delamere, Alice Sutherland-Hawes and the team at the Agency—it's been wonderful to collaborate with you on such an exciting project!

Thank you to my family, who coped beautifully with the news that I was going to be writing a surprise extra book, and who have supported me throughout the process. Special thanks go to my husband, David, who lived this book alongside me, and has listened patiently to me talk about everything from painting dimensions to the New York subway. There's no one who deserves this book more—I couldn't have done it without you by my side.

Thank you to my friends (sorry I was NEVER free for dinner—this book is why), and also to my author-support network: Non Pratt, Louie Stowell, Karen Lawler, Genn McMenemy, Charlie Morris (again), Anne Miller (again!) and every fantastic member of Team Cooper, who made sure I reached the finish line still basically cheerful and functioning. Thank you to Char, who gave me much-needed words of wisdom about first drafts. And finally, a shout-out to reader Wakiuru Wohoro, who named Sandra on Twitter.

Thank you to Natalie Doherty, Kelly Hurst, Harriet Venn, Francesca Dow, Tom Rawlinson, Sue Cook, Frances Evans and everyone else at Puffin, and thank you to Karen Greenberg and the team at Knopf for bringing Ted to America for real! And thank you to my agent, Gemma Cooper, for the years of hard work and resolve that have led to this amazing moment. Gemma, I am so glad to have you on my team!

The three books (apart from, of course, *The London Eye Mystery*) that deserve a special mention in the creation of *The Guggenheim Mystery* are *The Reason I Jump: The Inner Voice of a Thirteen-Year-Old Boy with Autism* by Naoki Higashida (translated by KA Yoshida and David Mitchell), which helped me get into the mind of Ted; *The Gardner Heist: The True Story of the World's Largest Unsolved Art Theft* by Ulrich Boser, which helped me understand the world of art theft; and *From the Mixed-Up Files of Mrs. Basil E. Frankweiler* by E. L. Konigsburg, which has been with me most of my life, and is my very favorite art-mystery story. Mrs. Basil E. runs through this story, even though I never managed to get Ted into the Met.

And finally, thank you to Siobhan. I wish I'd met you. I know we would have had a lot to talk about. Thank you for lending me Ted. I hope you liked this book.